LOVE AND CURSES

CRESCENT CITY GHOST TOURS

CARRIE PULKINEN

Love & Curses

Contact Information: www.CarriePulkinen.com

Cover Design by Rebecca Poole of Dreams2Media

First Edition, 2022
ISBN: 978-1-957253-05-3

CHAPTER ONE

*T*rish Bennet inhaled a breath of sultry summer air and gazed at the steamboat docked by the riverbank. The sun had begun its descent toward the horizon, its light reflecting off the muddy Mississippi, making the water sparkle as it sloshed against the side of the boat. The three-story, white wooden structure, which sported twin smokestacks and a massive red paddlewheel attached to the back, would hold her captive for the next three hours, forcing her to get to know her date, to give him a chance despite the missing spark of attraction she'd hoped to feel when she met him.

She didn't need fireworks, though. Sparks fizzled, and Trish was done with flashes in the pan.

"Got the tickets. Let's get this over with so we can get to the fun part, eh?" Kenneth wiggled his eyebrows and gestured toward the plank.

"This part will be fun too. Who doesn't love a good murder mystery?" She clutched her purse and stepped onto the boat as Kenneth chuckled, following behind her.

The man ticked all her boxes. Well, all except the spark

box, but that was the least important one. He was a successful criminal defense lawyer, so steady job: check. At thirty-seven years old, his age meant he'd achieved some level of maturity she hadn't found in the flings she'd occupied her time with over the past few years. Possibility of something long-term: check.

He was tall and somewhat handsome, with blonde hair, fair skin, pale blue eyes, and broad shoulders. Physical attraction: ...meh. But that was near the bottom of her list anyway. He'd made her laugh when they talked on the phone, and they had similar taste in music and movies, so this could work. Maybe.

Seventh time's the charm. Who knew finding love via online dating would be so hard?

Thick paisley-patterned carpet squished beneath her shoes as she stepped into the ballroom area, and she paused at the entrance, taking in the view. Art deco light fixtures hung evenly spaced along the white tile ceiling, and tables dressed in alabaster linen sat beneath the windows, creating an aisleway down the center of the long, rectangular space.

A small, raised platform stood in front of a wall of red curtains, and the hostess led them to a table in the front row, only a few feet away from the stage.

"Can we move to the back?" Kenneth jutted his thumb toward the rear of the ship as Trish sank into the seat offered her. "People in the front row always get heckled. I won't put up with being the butt of anyone's jokes."

"Umm…" The hostess scanned the seating chart. "Let me see what's available. It's a full ship tonight."

"This'll be fine." Trish patted the chair next to her. "It's a murder mystery show, not comedy."

Kenneth frowned and huffed, his shoulders slumping

as he dropped into the seat. "All right. Can I get a whiskey neat? Make it a double."

The hostess smiled and gestured to her left. "We have a cash bar right over there."

"What do you want?" Kenneth stood and tugged his wallet from his pocket.

"A glass of water would be nice."

"Don't make me drink alone."

Her jaw tightened as red flag number one raised in her mind. Trish had a tendency to lose her inhibitions when alcohol was involved, and she was trying her best to grow up and get her act together. Going home with him—or any man—on the first date was out of the question, despite her behavior in the past.

Kenneth looked at her expectantly, apparently not willing to take water for an answer. This was going to be a long night.

"I suppose one drink won't hurt. I'll have a glass of rosé if you don't mind."

"You got it." He grinned, revealing a dimple on his left cheek.

Trish loved a man with a dimple, but Kenneth's didn't make her stomach flutter. In fact, she didn't feel the slightest bit of…well, anything. Zero chemistry. Not an ounce of sizzle as she gazed at his backside while he walked toward the bar. He dropped his wallet and bent over to pick it up. Still nothing.

Oh, wait. Something in her stomach bubbled. Maybe she felt a little… Nope. She covered her mouth as she burped. The Dr Pepper she drank before she met Kenneth here was giving her more feelings than the man.

Oh, well. This cruise had rave reviews on Yelp for both the performance and the food. If the company was bad, at least she could enjoy the show. Kenneth returned with his whiskey and set a glass of red wine in front of Trish before typing on his phone.

"Thanks." She picked up the glass and sniffed the wine. It smelled rich and bold like a cabernet. "Were they out of rosé?"

"Huh?" He glanced up for a second and returned his gaze to the screen. "Oh, I thought you said red."

She waited for him to offer to exchange it for what she requested, but when he ignored her, she shrugged and took a sip. "Good thing I like red too." She might need a few more glasses to make it through the evening if this was how he was going to be.

Kenneth's blue text bubble floated on his screen, followed by several short responses from whomever he was texting. Trish wasn't close enough to read the exchange, but his posture stiffened, and he blew a hard breath through his nose.

"Everything okay?" she asked.

"Yeah." He slipped the phone into his pocket. "Arguing with my ex. It's a daily occurrence, so nothing to worry about."

"If she's your ex, why are you still arguing?"

"It's not important." He placed his hand on top of hers, and the clamminess of his sweaty palm made her shiver, but not in a good way.

She fought the urge to pull from his grasp. He was focusing on her now, so this was her opportunity to see if they had enough in common for a second date. "So, how do you like being a lawyer? Your job must be very exciting."

"It's all right. A lot of late nights, but the money is

worth it." His gaze dipped to her chest before returning to her eyes.

This time, she did pull from his grasp. "Sounds... interesting. I'm about to make a career change. I know my dating profile said I work at an urgent care clinic, but I'm about to buy a—"

His phone chimed. "Uh-huh. Hold on a minute." He took it from his pocket and scowled at the screen, mashing the keyboard with his thumbs.

Trish took a deep breath, trying to quell her frustration. Kenneth's behavior reminded her way too much of the way Connor, the man she followed to New Orleans a few years ago, used to treat her. Of course, she wouldn't have seen a red flag back then if it was flapping in her face. "Love is blind" was an understatement when it came to Trish in her twenties, but having her life uprooted and her heart torn out had made her cautious now. Maybe a little too cautious, but she was working on that.

So the seventh dating app prospect isn't the charm. Here's to number eight. She took a giant gulp of wine and focused her attention on the woman approaching the stage.

"Good evening, everyone." The announcer had deep-red hair styled into a pixie cut and a dark brown complexion. Her smile lit up her entire face, and as she opened her arms in a welcoming gesture, a pair of gold bracelets clinked on her wrist. "Welcome to a night of fun, good food, and of course...murder. We'll start with dinner, and once the main course is done, our fabulous emcee will guide you through the sordid tale of an heiress killed in cold blood. Who did it? That's for *you* to figure out."

As the woman exited the stage, waiters scurried about, delivering food and filling glasses with sweet tea. Kenneth finally put his phone away, but he seemed distracted through dinner, giving short answers to Trish's questions and hardly looking at her. His body may have been on a date with her, but his mind was somewhere else entirely.

"Do you want to talk about it?" Trish set down her fork and folded her hands in her lap.

He grinned. "I'm not going to talk about my ex while I'm on a date with my future ex."

You'll just spend the entire night arguing with her via text. Classy. Trish smirked at his ill-planned joke and returned her attention to the food, the only good thing about this date so far.

The shrimp and grits came with a creamy cheese sauce that melted in her mouth. Who knew a breakfast food would pair so well with shellfish? She savored each bite, scraping the bottom of her bowl to scoop up every last bit before the server cleared the table and the show began.

Kenneth rested an arm on the back of her chair, and she leaned forward, folding hers on the table. The lights in the dining room dimmed as a spotlight shined on the curtains, and a man stepped onto the tiny stage.

Trish's lips parted on a quick intake of air, and her heart kicked into a sprint. The sizzle she *hadn't* felt for any of her past seven dates flared to life, her lips curving into a smile as she swept her gaze over the alluring man.

Eric Landry looked scrumptious in black pants, a matching blazer, and a white collared shirt with the top two buttons casually undone. He had short, dark brown hair and bright hazel eyes, and the neatly trimmed beard he'd grown since she last saw him added a matureness to his already sexy vibe.

Talk about checking her spark box. *Yum.*

Attraction wasn't the issue when it came to Eric Landry. He'd starred in plenty of Trish's fantasies since she met him three years ago, and, judging by the way his eyes sparkled as she caught his gaze, the feeling was mutual.

There were two problems when it came to Eric. One: he worked for Crescent City Ghost Tours, a group of people who had become her primary circle of friends over the years since her bestie married their leader. Dating within the friend group was never a good idea. Sure, it might have worked out in the long run for Monica and Chandler, and even Ross and Rachel, but this wasn't a TV show and the fictional couples had run into more issues along the way than Trish cared to endure.

Problem number two: Eric was young and wild. Okay, wild wasn't really an issue. Trish was plenty wild herself in her younger years, but if she was just stepping off the fast train at thirty, Eric still had miles and miles to go. He was only twenty-four years old, and for the first time since the reason she moved to New Orleans dumped her, Trish was looking for more than a fling.

"Good evening, ladies and gentlemen. My name is Eric Landry," his strong, confident voice commanded attention, making Trish's stomach flutter. "'Detective' Landry, that is." He made air quotes. "I don't want you to be alarmed, but there's been a murder aboard this boat tonight, and someone in this very room is the culprit." He waved an arm at the audience dramatically, and a few patrons giggled. The man knew how to work a crowd.

"This is my assistant, Amy." He gestured toward the woman stepping onto the stage. "She's going to give many of you a folder with the part you'll play in this investigation. Raise your hand if you'd like to volunteer."

Trish started to lift her hand, but Kenneth's groan stopped her. Honestly, why did the guy agree to come here at all if he was going to act this way? She'd simply suggested it when he asked where she wanted to go for their first date. He could have said no.

Amy picked up a pile of brown folders and distributed them to the volunteers. Eric grinned and tugged one from her grasp before dropping it on the table in front of Trish. "I've got the perfect part for you."

"We're good, man." Kenneth palmed the folder and slid it back toward Eric before Trish could even touch it. "And no heckling either. We didn't ask for the front row."

Eric cocked his head, cutting his gaze between them. "Is that what the lady wants?"

Trish cleared her throat and forced a smile. "It's fine, Eric. Thank you, but I'll pass."

He gave her a pointed look, and she could only imagine the array of questions tumbling through his mind, the first one probably being, "Why the hell are you out with this guy?"

Good question, Eric. In-Person-Kenneth was nothing like the man she'd spoken to on the phone. Whatever charisma he'd exhibited then must've been fabricated because this guy didn't possess an ounce of charm. But she still had another two hours to endure with him, so she'd save telling him off for the end.

"Are you sure?" Eric asked.

She nodded. "Maybe next time."

As Eric picked up the folder and handed it to Amy, Kenneth scoffed. "We're not doing this again, sweetheart. From now on, I pick the place."

There's not going to be a next time for you, buddy. She bit her tongue to stop from saying the words aloud. Kenneth didn't seem like the kind of guy who took rejection well. Short of secretly throwing him overboard, she couldn't imagine a way of dumping him that wouldn't cause a scene.

Eric frowned, clearly disappointed in her choice of company for the evening, and he ascended the stage. Kenneth grunted, returning his attention to his precious phone, and Eric caught her gaze. She smiled, which she tended to do around him anyway, and mouthed the words *I'm fine.*

His grin returned as he nodded once and began the show. "Our adventure begins in a Garden District mansion, about fifteen minutes outside the French Quarter. The heiress, Elizabeth Dupuis, was taking tea in the garden when her young life was cut short."

The mention of a mansion caught Trish's attention, and as she watched Eric orchestrate the show, she all but forgot about her poor choice in dates. At least Kenneth had the courtesy to hold his phone in his lap as he typed, making his annoyance with the situation slightly less obvious.

Eric wove a fascinating tale of mystery, coaching the audience members as they read from their scripts, and Trish was mesmerized by his performance. Though she saw him occasionally at group gatherings over the years, they weren't much more than casual acquaintances. She had no idea he'd be running the show when she suggested this event to Kenneth. She didn't know much about Eric at all, to be honest.

Sure, they flirted like crazy whenever they were together, but Trish always kept her distance when the group outing ended, rushing off before things could get awkward. Come to think of it, she'd never actually been alone with him for more than ten minutes to have any sort of getting-to-know-you type of conversation.

That was probably a good thing. With the way her body reacted to the man, she'd end up in bed with him faster than she could blink, and she was *so* not going there with Eric. It would ruin their whole dynamic.

Besides, Eric was an empath, and though he swore Trish was immune to his emotional prying ability, the last thing she needed was a man who had access to her innermost feelings and desires. Her anxiety disorder was her own, thank you very much.

She glanced at Kenneth, who rolled his eyes and made a crude gesture with his hands as if his opinion of the dinner theater wasn't obvious before. Now that she thought about it, the last thing she needed was the hassle of a man at all. With her upcoming career change, she was about to be too busy anyway.

"And now," Eric's commanding voice drew her attention. "As you contemplate who you think was the culprit, we'll take a break for my favorite part of the evening. Dessert."

"I think it was her brother. Who do you—?"

Kenneth's phone rang, and he snatched it off the table. "I need to take this. Don't eat my cake while I'm gone." Knocking his chair back, he shot to his feet and disappeared through the door leading to the dining room balcony.

Trish shook her head. *What an asshole.*

Her bread pudding with white chocolate sauce was divine and paired perfectly with the café au lait the waitress served. Eric made his way toward her, but patron after patron stopped him to discuss the mystery. By the time he made it to her table, she'd finished dessert, but Kenneth remained on the balcony outside.

"Your date seems like an interesting fellow. Where'd he run off to?"

Trish gestured to the door. "He's outside, probably talking to his ex."

He cringed. "I hope he cuts ties with the baggage before your next date."

"This'll be our last. I don't have time to waste with a man who can't be present in the moment."

"Good call. You know, if you went out with me, you'd have my undivided attention." Heat sparked in his gaze, and her stomach fluttered again.

"I'm sure I would. Sadly, I'm more woman than you could handle."

"Try me."

"You'd like that." God, she loved their flirting game.

"Damn right I would." He laughed. "Where'd you meet that guy, anyway?"

"Online dating site."

"I see. Well, better luck next time."

"Yeah, I think I've had enough cyber connections for a while. I'm buying my own mansion, so that's going to take up most of my time as soon as the sale goes through."

"A mansion?" His brows lifted. "I didn't know you were in the market for something like that."

"There's a lot you don't know about me."

He pulled out Kenneth's chair and sat down. "And that's a shame. Tell me about it."

"Eric…" Amy patted his shoulder as she walked by. "Show's on."

His gaze never strayed from Trish's eyes. "Give me a minute. Trish was about to tell me about her recent purchase."

"Well, it's not final." She tucked her hair behind her

ear, suddenly embarrassed at the thought of discussing her financial situation with him. She could only afford the down payment on the place because she finally had control of her trust fund. There was no reason to be ashamed about that. It was her money to do with what she liked, and she'd worked her ass off to prove she deserved it...both to herself and to the wicked stepmother who made sure Trish knew she'd never amount to anything.

She ground her teeth. Her dysfunctional family was a rabbit hole her thoughts did not need to tumble down tonight. Trish was finally out from under that woman's unrelenting thumb, and her life was coming together splendidly. No need to ruin it with ruminations.

"We have to stay on schedule. You can chat after." Amy jerked her head toward the stage, and Eric sighed.

"Let's talk later, okay?" He squeezed Trish's hand before rising to his feet and ascending the steps to the stage.

Her palm still warm from his touch, she folded her hands in her lap and breathed deeply to slow her heart. They weren't lacking in the chemistry department, that was for sure.

Halfway through the big reveal, Kenneth finally graced them with his presence. He took two bites of his dessert and shoved it away, impatiently drumming his fingers on the table.

The show ended as the boat pulled into the dock, and the patrons shook Eric's hand, congratulating him on a good performance. Kenneth gripped the back of Trish's neck with a clammy palm and leaned toward her ear. "I'm ready for the *real* dessert now, sweetheart."

Ew. The line to disembark was slow-moving, so Trish excused herself to the restroom to avoid any more unwelcome advances. Her stomach soured as she gazed at her reflection in the mirror, and she focused on her breathing to stave off the anxiety threatening to tip into panic. She'd dealt with men like this before, and it was best to send him packing when she actually had the ability to get away.

When she returned to the dining area, most of the passengers had left the ship, and she found Kenneth standing near the exit, talking to Eric.

"You know women," Kenneth said as she approached from behind. "If you lay them right the first time, you can walk all over them the rest of their lives."

She stopped, her mouth falling open, as Eric's jaw tightened. He looked at her, and Kenneth turned around, following his gaze.

"There you are, babe." He clutched the back of her neck possessively again. "Do you need a ride back to your place, or should I follow you?"

Her muscles crawled beneath her skin as she stepped out of his grasp and stood next to Eric. "This isn't going to work for me, Kenneth. It's best if we go our separate ways now."

Kenneth gaped before narrowing his eyes. "The night is young. Don't leave me hanging."

She crossed her arms, and he moved toward her. "I paid for your ticket and your wine," he growled. "You owe me. Let's go."

"I'm not going anywhere with you."

"The hell you aren't." He grabbed her arm, his fingers digging into her bicep, and half a second later, Eric's fist connected with his jaw.

CHAPTER TWO

*K*enneth careened backward, tumbling over a table and hitting his head on the edge of a chair. Eric half-expected Trish to run to the guy's side to make sure he was okay, but she just stood there, eyes wide, her gaze darting between him and her date.

His empathic ability was useless on Trish, so he had no idea what she was feeling. He had managed to redirect Kenneth's anger at her for refusing to take him home to himself, so there was that.

"Son of a bitch." Kenneth scrambled to his feet and wiped the blood from his lip. The sharp sting of shock, burning embarrassment, and the scratchy feel of fear that he'd lost control of the situation formed the base of the anger that slammed into Eric, nearly knocking him off his feet.

Damn, this guy had strong emotions.

As Kenneth moved toward him, Eric slid in front of Trish, intent on taking the brunt of the asshole's anger. "I suggest you walk away before you make things worse."

Kenneth narrowed his eyes and let out a sardonic

laugh. "Things are about to get a lot worse…for you." He raised his voice. "Who's in charge? I want the police here. Now."

Trish gripped Eric's arm, and he opened up his senses, trying desperately to detect a hint of her emotions. Was she relieved? Scared? Pissed? He had no idea, and he didn't dare turn around to look at her with the rage still rolling off Kenneth's body.

Chantel strode toward them, concern furrowing her brow. "I'm the manager. Is there a problem?" She gasped as she took in Kenneth's busted lip.

"I was trying to leave with my date, and this clown punched me. I want an officer here; I'm pressing charges."

"Eric, is that true?" Chantel flashed an incredulous look.

"He was…" Grinding his teeth, he glanced at Trish before focusing on his boss. He shouldn't have done that. Trish was a woman who could take care of herself. Of that he was certain. "Yes, it's true."

Chantel crossed her arms. "Well, I hope you had a good reason."

"He was trying to protect me." Trish rested a hand on his shoulder, and he tensed. "I didn't want to leave with him…" She gestured at her date. "He grabbed my arm, and Eric must have thought he was going to hurt me."

Kenneth scoffed. "I wasn't going to hurt you, babe. I just wanted to get you away from this asshole. He's a loose cannon. He could've just as easily hurt you."

Eric's hands clenched into fists, and he instinctively loomed toward the bastard. Trish's firm grip on his shoulder was the only thing stopping him from landing another punch.

"Okay." Chantel stepped between them. "Eric, my

office. Now." She turned to Kenneth. "I am deeply sorry for what happened…"

Trish bit her lip as he turned and paced toward Chantel's small office. "Eric…" She lifted a hand as if reaching for him.

"I'm sorry." He stepped into the room and closed the door.

What the hell had he just done? His ears burned with embarrassment, and his stomach churned with unease as he sank into a chair. He'd made an ass of himself in front of a smart, sophisticated woman, and whatever "might-be" relationship he'd dreamed of having with Trish turned into "what might have been."

He'd let his emotions get the better of him, and he shouldn't have. He was a goddamn empath, for Pete's sake. Emotional control was a requirement for keeping his sanity. Otherwise, the constant barrage of other people's feelings would send him on a downward spiral that only a straight-jacket and a padded cell could help.

But the moment he saw that asshole's fingers dig into Trish's arm, he'd lost it. He'd let Kenneth's emotions mingle with his own, and the result was a pop to the jaw he could never take back.

He sat there stewing in remorse for another fifteen minutes before Chantel opened the door and slipped inside. She took the chair next to him, shaking her head as she inhaled deeply and sighed.

"What happened out there, Eric?"

"He was getting rough with her. He grabbed her arm, and he wanted to hit her. So…I hit him first."

She pursed her lips and studied his eyes. "Did he raise a hand to her? Did he threaten her?"

"Not outright, but he wanted to."

"And you knew he wanted to, how?"

His nostrils flared as he blew out a breath. "I just knew. You could see it in his eyes." His ability wasn't something he shared with most people. Psychic powers were often misunderstood, and he'd been called crazy enough in his life. His gift of reading the emotions of others frightened people.

Chantel nodded, clasping her hands in her lap. "He agreed not to press charges."

"That's a relief."

"On one condition. We have to let you go." The look in her eyes was one of sympathy, but regret billowed in her aura like smoke. She hated to let him go. Eric was the reason they had a full ship twice a month for every murder mystery theater. "I'm so sorry."

And then he felt it…her inevitable disappointment slapped him across the face, shattering what little pride he'd managed to hold onto. He'd let her down, let the entire staff down. And Trish? She'd probably never speak to him again after that little display of immaturity.

Dusting off his pants, he stood and stepped around her chair. "I am too, but that seems like a fair trade."

"Your final paycheck will be deposited next week."

"Thanks." He pulled the door shut behind him, shoved his hands into his pockets, and made his way down the gangplank toward the parking lot.

"Eric!" Trish's voice drifted on the summer breeze, and he turned to find her shutting the door of her Toyota and jogging toward him.

His breath caught at the sight of her prancing across the parking lot, her heels clicking on the asphalt as her knee-length sunflower dress swished with each stride. Her short blonde hair glinted in the moonlight, and she stopped two feet in front of him, tucking a strand behind her ear.

"What happened in there?" Her voice held concern rather than annoyance or anger, and the knot in his stomach loosened.

"Do you mean why did I hit him? Or what happened after I was sent to the office like a naughty schoolboy?"

Her red lips curved into a tiny smile. "I know why you hit him. He's an asshole. The bartender escorted me to my car while your boss tried to calm Kenneth down. Is he pressing charges?"

"No, he agreed not to."

"Oh, thank goodness." Her posture relaxed as she stepped toward him.

"In exchange for me being fired."

"You got fired?" She bit her bottom lip.

He shrugged. "Between that and going to jail, I think it's a fair trade. I'm sorry I hit your boyfriend."

She shook her head. "He's not. That was our first and last date, and... Can I buy you a drink? I feel like *I* need to apologize for even bringing him on the ship. I'm sorry you got fired."

A drink? Now there was an unexpected twist. If she was disappointed in the way he acted, she didn't show it outwardly, and what a relief that was. Very few people were impervious to his ability. In fact, he could probably count them all on his fingers. It was so damn refreshing to talk to someone without being privy to their innermost feelings. Trish's immunity was only one of the countless things he found attractive about her.

"You don't need to apologize for a choice I made, but I would love a drink...especially with the company of a beautiful woman."

"Hmm…" She grinned slyly. "Are you sure you'll be okay? You might spontaneously combust from spending time in the presence of this much hotness."

He laughed. "If it's my time to go, I've lived a good life. I'll take my chances."

They walked side by side out of the parking lot and crossed Decatur Street before heading into a bar. The buzz of a dozen different emotions—none of them his own—scratched his skin like sandpaper as they made their way toward a small table in the back of the room. With a deep inhale, he drew his empathic energy inward, creating a metaphysical bubble of protection around himself and blocking out the silent chatter.

He pulled out a chair and stood behind it, and Trish cocked her head. He slid it out a little more. "I'm nothing if not a gentleman." His grandmother made sure of that.

She accepted the gesture, and he scooted the chair forward as she sank into it. "This isn't a date." She picked up the cocktail menu. "It's one apology drink, and then I have to get home."

"Understood." He sat across from her. "I can't help the way I was raised."

A server arrived, and Trish ordered a glass of rosé. Eric quickly scanned the menu before laying it on the table. "I'll have the same."

The server took the menus, and Trish arched a brow at him. "I didn't peg you for a wine drinker."

"Oh? What would you guess my signature drink would be?"

She leaned back in the chair and studied him. "You're barely out of college, so I would guess tequila shots or Jägermeister."

He straightened his spine. "I graduated two years ago. I'm a little more sophisticated than that."

"I'm pretty sure I've seen you shoot Patron with Jason." Her smile was playful, but her opinion of him stung. Yes, there was a bit of an age gap between them, but his maturity was beyond his years. It had to be, lest he become the disappointment his mother always felt he was.

Okay, punching her date wasn't the most grown-up thing he could have done, but who knew what that guy might've done if he'd followed her outside? It was no secret Eric had the hots for Trish from the moment they met. He flirted with her every chance he got, and she always returned the sentiment. But any suggestion of them going on an actual date was always met with a playful rejection. She didn't take him seriously, and his actions tonight didn't help his case.

"And I'm pretty sure I've seen you shoot buttery nipples with Sydney. Shots serve their purpose, but having a single apology drink with a friend isn't the time."

She pressed her lips together as the server delivered their drinks. Lifting her glass in a toast, she cleared her throat. "You make a good point. To friendship and apologies."

He lifted his glass and clinked it on hers. "And to forgiveness."

"To forgiveness." She took a sip before setting her glass on the table. "How long did you work on the steamboat before I came along and got you fired?"

"I got myself fired, but I'd worked there about eight months."

"What are you going to do now? Can you pick up more shifts with the tour company to make up for the loss of income?"

He chuckled. Income was the least of his worries, though his finances and upcoming inheritance weren't things he openly discussed. Nobody liked a spoiled a rich kid. "I wasn't going to work there much longer anyway. I'm planning to open my own murder mystery dinner theater in an old family property."

"That sounds exciting. Tell me about it."

His smile widened. "You know how the Landry mansion has been in my family from the beginning? It's where I grew up."

"I do. I still need to go out there for a tour someday."

"I'm happy to show you around anytime. You don't have to shuffle through with the tourists."

"Hmm…and would that private tour happen to end in your old bedroom?"

He chuckled. "Only if you want it to."

She caught her bottom lip between her teeth, and a flash of heat sparked in her eyes. "I'd ruin you for other women. It wouldn't be fair." She sipped her wine. "So you're going to do the shows at your family home?"

"My grandma just acquired a piece of property that had been lost to gambling debts a century ago. It needs a little of TLC before I can open shop, but it's a dream come true."

"That does sound like a dream come true. In fact, we might be neighbors."

He cocked his head. "Your mansion?"

"It's not nearly as big as Landry House, but it has a garden area that will be gorgeous once I'm done with it. The seller accepted my offer, and I'm just waiting for the loan to get approved. I'm going to run it as a bed and breakfast."

"Really?" He leaned his elbow on the table, drifting toward her. "I didn't peg you for the homebody type."

She smirked. "Running a B and B is a bit different from staying home all the time in sweatpants with no bra."

Now there was a sight he'd like to see. He could imagine her sitting on the porch swing, drinking coffee while he tossed a ball to the dog in their front yard. Okay, maybe he was getting a little ahead of himself. Still, it was a lovely thought.

"I'll be up before dawn preparing breakfast for my guests," her voice drew him from his daydream, "attending to their rooms when they leave for the day, and doing all kinds of other stuff to keep the place running."

"Sounds like a dream come true."

"It is. I've wanted to run my own business for as long as I can remember. Working at the urgent care clinic is okay, but it's not what I want to do for the rest of my life. I'm thirty. It's time I grew up, quit my job, and started my career."

"I'm so glad it's coming together for you. I guess you worked in hospitality before the urgent care? A restaurant or hotel?"

"Well, no, but I've eaten in plenty of restaurants and stayed in my share of hotels."

Wow. That was quite an endeavor, investing in a property without any experience in the type of business she planned to run. "I can tell you're excited about it."

"Oh? So your empathic abilities do work on me." Her sly smile affected his pulse.

He chuckled. "I don't need psychic abilities to see your enthusiasm. Your eyes sparkle when you talk about it." So far be it from him to burst her bubble. He'd keep his opinion on her lack of experience to himself.

"You…" She held his gaze, and something about her expression changed. It was subtle, almost imperceptible, but Eric had spent years studying body language and facial expressions, trying to figure out why he just *knew* things about people. It wasn't until he started ghost hunting and could feel the emotions of spirits that he realized he had a psychic ability.

Trish's eyes softened, her brows tugging together and lifting slightly like she was *seeing* him for the first time. "Thanks for listening. I'm sure Emily is tired of my rambling. I can't stop talking about it." She let out a nervous laugh and polished off the rest of her wine.

"I can't wait to hear more when the sale goes through, and hey… If you ever want any pointers, my grandma would love to sit down with you. She's been running a B and B for decades."

"Thanks. I might take you up on that. Do you mind if we close?" She flagged down the server. "I work an early shift tomorrow."

"No problem." He reached for his wallet out of habit, but Trish slipped the server her credit card before he could remove it from his pocket.

"I told you I was buying. I'm really sorry about your job. Your show was very good."

"I appreciate that. It'll be even better when I open my theater."

"I'll be sure to suggest it to my guests." She signed the receipt and returned her card to her purse. "And I'll be there opening night."

"I'll save a seat for you in the front row."

They sat there for a beat or two, looking at each other, before she stood and slipped her purse strap onto her shoulder. "It was good seeing you."

"We should have lunch sometime since we'll be working in the same area." He knew what her answer would be. He'd lost count of how many times he'd asked her out, but he had to try.

She tilted her head. "Bye, Eric."

Shot down again, as he expected. "See you around, Trish."

CHAPTER THREE

*T*rish signed out of her computer and tugged her purse from the drawer. "I don't know why Madeline hasn't called me about a closing date. The loan went through this morning."

Emily leaned on the counter in the urgent care reception room, her long red hair spilling around her shoulders as she looked at her friend. "Do you want me to call her? She took Sable to the park this morning, and she tends to get carried away with her granddaughter."

"No, I don't want any special treatment from my BFF's mother-in-law. It'll be that much sweeter when this all comes together if I don't take any easy ways out."

Emily rested her chin on her fist. "I sure am going to miss seeing your beautiful face all the time."

Pressure built in the back of Trish's eyes as she took a deep breath. The clean scents of soap and antiseptic filled her senses, and a heaviness settled in her chest. "Don't get all sappy on me, Em. We'll still be besties; I'm just moving on to my dream job, not moving towns."

"I'm proud of you."

Her throat thickened. "Thanks, but it's not that big of a deal."

"It's a huge deal. You came to New Orleans following a man who dumped you a week after you moved. You worked two jobs while going to school to learn medical billing, and you were hired here at the clinic as soon as you earned your certificate."

Trish lifted a shoulder, and heat crept up her neck to spread across her cheeks. "What else was I going to do? Adrienne had control of my purse strings, and she zipped the damn thing shut when I moved."

"You could have run back to Houston with your tail between your legs. It's probably what I would have done."

"Whatever. You've been through a lot worse and came out better in spite of it." All Trish had to do was make it to thirty. Her stepmother was in charge of the money her father had left to her until then, and Adrienne was furious it didn't all belong to her. She wasn't about to let Trish have a dime when she decided to move to New Orleans one day and packed her bags the same night.

All for that asshole Connor and the happily ever after she'd assumed he'd give her. Trish had asked herself what she'd been thinking hundreds of times since she uprooted her life for a man who had the maturity of a hyena, and the answer was always the same. She hadn't been thinking at all. "Young and dumb" didn't begin to describe Trish back then, but things had changed. *She* had changed.

Rising to her feet, she slipped her purse strap onto her shoulder, and her phone buzzed from inside. Her heart pounded as she gripped the device. "Eek! It's Madeline. I'll put it on speaker." She tapped the screen. "Hello?"

"Good afternoon, Trish. How are you?" Her voice held a hint of wariness.

Trish snapped her gaze to Emily, and her friend tightened her eyes. *Oh, no.* Her heart plopped into her stomach, taking most of the blood from her head with it. She rested her hand on the counter to steady herself, her jaw tightening as she spoke, "I'll be much better when you tell me the good news. When am I closing?"

Madeline didn't just miss a beat in her reply; she was silent for a full three seconds. "I'm sorry, Trish. Another buyer came in with a cash offer, and the seller accepted. We'll keep looking though. I heard a rumor there's a mansion in Tremé that might be going on the market soon. It would make a beautiful bed and breakfast."

Her hands trembled, so she set the phone on the counter and sank into the chair. "They can't do that, can they? They'd already accepted my offer."

"The other buyer made a better one."

"But they didn't give me a chance to counter." This couldn't be happening. Everything about this had been so perfect. Trish had read an article about a couple who'd renovated an old mansion and turned it into a B and B a few weeks ago. She'd known right then that it was the perfect career for her, exactly what she wanted to spend her money on. She'd called Madeline the next day, and the Garden District mansion had gone on the market shortly after.

"This happens sometimes, dear. They were offered cash, and they took it rather than chance your financing falling through."

"My loan was approved this morning."

"I'm so sorry. The deal already closed."

A lump the size of a baseball formed in her throat, and she forced the words over it. "Thanks for letting me know."

"I'll call you the moment I find something else. Talk soon."

"Bye, Madeline." She mashed her finger on the phone to end the call and dropped her elbows on the counter with a *thunk.* "Well, crap."

Emily padded around and sank into the chair next to her before wrapping her arm around her shoulders. "I'm so sorry. That really sucks."

The pressure that had built in her eyes at the thought of leaving her job with her bestie now turned to tears gathering on her lower lids. "I can't believe they bought it out from under me."

"The bastards."

"Right? Who does that?" She wiped her eyes. "They can't just swoop in like some entitled ass and take my house. I've saved every penny I could for years. My credit is spotless. Just because I don't have that much cash on hand doesn't mean I shouldn't get to live my dream."

Emily rubbed her back. "I'm sure Madeline will find something else for you. She knows places are going to be for sale days before they hit the market. It's like a sixth sense."

"I know. That's how she found this place. I made my offer the day it was listed, but places like that aren't sold very often. It could be years before she finds something else."

"What about the mansion in Tremé?"

Trish shrugged. "I really wanted a Garden District house. Something with a little more space so I could have gardens for people to walk through, get married in."

"I'm sorry. But, hey, the good news is we haven't hired your replacement yet, so you can keep working here as long as you need to. More time to save means you'll have a bigger down payment for the next one."

"If there is a next one."

"There will be." Emily folded her hands in her lap, and concern drew her brows together. "Maybe…maybe this is a good thing. It'll give you more time to think about it, do some research, and make sure it's really what you want to do. You did make this decision on a whim."

"It wasn't on a whim. I've always wanted to be my own boss."

"But is a B and B the business you want to run?"

"Yes, Em. It is." Sure, she'd made the decision quickly, but it wasn't reckless or rash like so many she'd made before. It felt right, so she'd acted. Good things didn't come to those who waited; they came to those who put themselves out there and did the work.

"Okay. Then I support you one hundred percent."

The bell chimed, and Mindy, the afternoon office staff, strode through the door. "And? When's the big day?"

"Never," Trish grumbled and stuffed her phone into her purse.

"Don't say that." Emily stood and made her way around the counter as Mindy stepped into the office area. "The deal fell through, but there will be another house."

"That sucks." Mindy sank into a chair and rolled toward the computer before logging in.

"Tell me about it," Trish said. "I'm heading home."

Her bestie gave her a sympathetic look. "How about I stop by this evening? Sean will be home around five, so he can watch Sable, and I'll be at your place by five-thirty."

"That's okay. Pity parties are a single's event."

"Everything is going to work out in time." Emily smiled softly. "You'll see."

Trish nodded and headed out the door. Her stomach churned as she climbed into her car and started the engine. Time was one thing she no longer had.

Emily didn't know it, but Trish's lease was up at the end of the month and she'd been so excited when the owners accepted her offer, she hadn't renewed. The landlord had already promised it to a new tenant, so Trish would be moving no matter what. And good luck finding a place on such short notice. Her apartment building had a months-long waiting list. Most did.

It wasn't the first snap decision—AKA mistake—she'd made, and it wouldn't be the last. She'd figure something out, though; she always did. Tonight would be her one night to wallow in self-pity; then she'd put on her big girl britches and get on with her life.

After parking in the apartment lot, she walked two blocks to the local grocery store for her pity party supplies. A bottle of merlot and a wedge of brie would go nicely with her whine, so she gathered them and a pack of water crackers into a hand-held basket and made her way to the cashier.

"Hey, Trish." Carissa pushed her glasses up her nose before running the crackers across the scanner. "Uh oh. It's been a while since you've had a wine and cheese night. Everything okay?"

"I'm sure it will be eventually." She forced a smile and paid for her groceries. Damn, she would miss this neighborhood. Everyone was so friendly.

"If you need anything else, give me a call. I get off at eight, and I can bring it by your house on my way home."

"Thanks, Carissa. I appreciate that." Trish headed home and climbed the steps to her second-floor apartment. After dropping her dinner in the kitchen, she went to her bedroom and changed out of her scrubs and into a pair of black shorts and a white tank.

She glanced at the clock. It was only three p.m. If she opened the wine now, she'd be in bed by six. She was *way* too young for a night like that, so she shuffled to the living room and plopped onto the couch.

Flipping through the channels, she settled on *Love It or List It*, which used to be her favorite show. Big mistake. Watching the realtor take the couple around to all those huge houses made acid bubble in her stomach.

It was pointless to be angry. Dwelling on it would only make her feel worse, but she couldn't help it. Some rich prick probably wanted a trophy mansion he would only use twice a year. He'd ripped Trish's dream right out from under her, and for what? So he would have a place to stay during Mardi Gras and Jazzfest?

"Dickwad," she grumbled as she mashed the off button on the remote. That house was perfect. She already knew how she'd decorate every nook and cranny of the place. The small ballroom would make an ideal gathering space for wedding receptions, and with eight bedrooms, she could take one for herself and rent out the rest.

I bet he's there right now, telling some contractor about all the upgrades he wants to make. He'll rip out the original fixtures to make it "livable" even though he isn't going to live there.

She ground her teeth until sharp pain shot from her jaw to her temple. No, she didn't know for certain the rich prick wasn't going to live there. Hell, she didn't even know if a man bought the place—or if he was a prick—but there was one way to find out.

She shot to her feet and grabbed her shoes, slipping them on before clutching her purse and darting out the door. Her pulse raced as she descended the steps and made her way to the parking lot, a nagging voice in her head telling her she needed to calm the eff down and think this through.

What did she plan to do when she got there? Knock on the door and introduce herself? What would be the point of that? *C'mon, Trish. What are you doing?*

She climbed into her car and slammed the door. "I'll just drive by, see what kind of car is parked there, and then I'll let it go." With a nod, she pressed the button to start the engine and then pulled onto the road.

It took half an hour to drive to the Garden District, which should have been plenty of time for her to realize she was only rubbing salt into her wound by doing this. She should have turned around and gone back home to her wine and cheese, but as she reached St. Charles Avenue and took in the splendor of the Victorian and Colonial mansions with their grand columns and pristinely manicured yards, she couldn't help herself. She had to see her almost-home one more time.

It wasn't the largest or the grandest mansion on the block, but as she rolled to a stop near the curb, her chest tightened at the sight of it. The pale yellow two-story had dark green shutters and a front gallery trimmed in matching cast iron. Another gallery wrapped around the right side of the structure, reaching all the way to the back bedroom—the one Trish had planned to make her own.

A green fence with cast iron cornstalk posts blocked the yard from passersby on the sidewalk, and even though the home had sat vacant for nearly forty years, the grounds were immaculate with perfectly trimmed hedges, an enormous oak towering on the left, and a gorgeous magnolia tree with massive white blooms standing on the right.

Whoever had owned the house cared about appearances. Or maybe the homeowners' association breathed down their neck until they kept the outside in impeccable condition. Madeline had taken Trish through the inside a few days ago. It was dusty, everything covered in drop cloths, but some of the furniture would be useable. Not the waterbed in the main bedroom for sure, but they had a few period pieces.

Trish parked on the road and stepped onto the sidewalk. The gated driveway stood open, and a silver Mazda was parked near the house. Not what she was expecting the rich prick to drive, but that didn't mean anything.

Movement in the front window caught her eye, and she froze at the end of the driveway, her hands curling into fists as she fought the overwhelming urge to get a closer look at the person inside. *That's called trespassing, Trish. Don't do it.*

Then again, the gate was open. If she got caught, she could always say she was chasing her cat. She didn't own an animal, but one little peek at the person who stole her dream wouldn't hurt. "Bad decision, girl. This is *so* bad." She tip-toed up the driveway.

A silhouette filled the window—definitely male with broad shoulders and short hair—so she darted to the side of the house. Her heart galloped in her chest as she pressed her back against the wall, and her rational mind finally tried to overpower her emotions.

This was up there with the top five biggest mistakes she'd ever made. She could get arrested for doing this…or shot. "Gah! I'm an idiot." She clamped her hand over her mouth. No need to announce her presence to the guy as she slunk through his yard like a criminal.

With her eyes fixed on the sidewalk, her muscles

tensed as she prepared to escape. But when a shadow passed by the nearest window, she really, truly couldn't help herself. A wooden box sat beneath the pane, practically inviting her to take a peek inside.

She softly planted one foot on the edge of the box and shifted her weight. When it didn't give, she gripped the sill and hoisted herself up, squatting beneath the window. Her pulse felt like a pair of hummingbird wings beating against her ribs, and her palms slicked with sweat.

Slowly, quietly, she lifted her head and peered through the thick glass. Though he faced away from her, she would recognize that backside anywhere because she had spent plenty of time admiring it, imagining what it would look like minus the form-fitting jeans.

"What the actual eff?" Eric Landry was the rich prick who'd bought *her* house? "Son of a bitch!"

He turned toward the window, and her foot slipped from the box. She squealed and gripped the ledge, but gravity got the better of her and yanked her down. Her chin smacked the sill on her way to the ground, and the unforgiving concrete promised an array of bruises on her back. Sharp pain shot from her shoulder to her spine, and as she rose to sit, clutching the back of her head, Eric ran out the front door.

"Trish? Holy crap. Are you okay?" He kneeled by her side and brushed the hair from her face. It was a tender gesture, and if she wasn't furious with him, it might have given her the warm fuzzies.

Instead, she knocked his hand away. "I'm fine."

He peered at her chin. "You're bleeding."

"It's nothing." She clambered to her feet and dusted off her butt, a million questions and accusations swirling in her mind, forming a knot in her throat.

"Why don't you come inside and let me get you a bandage? You'll drip all over your white shirt."

It would be best not to give him a piece of her mind out here in the yard for all the neighbors to hear, so she stomped up the front steps and crossed her arms.

His smirk, which normally sent a thrill shimmying up her spine, fueled her irritation, and as he ascended onto the porch and opened the door, she dug her nails into her biceps to keep from throttling him.

Okay, she wouldn't have actually choked the man, but she was tempted, nonetheless.

She followed him into the foyer, down the long hallway toward the kitchen, where he ran a paper towel under the faucet. He'd owned the house less than twenty-four hours, and he'd already removed the drop cloths and had the electricity and water reconnected. *Figures. His family has all kinds of money.*

She ground her teeth as he dabbed the wet towel on her chin. It stung, but she wasn't about to show weakness in front of him. He handed her a dry towel, and she pressed it against the wound as he opened a plastic first aid kit and pulled out a small bandage.

"It's just a little scrape. I don't think stitches will be required." He had the nerve to chuckle as he applied the bandage to her skin. "What are you doing here…and why were you climbing onto a box outside?"

She finally found her voice. "What am *I* doing here?" She scoffed. "What are *you* doing here?"

He threw the bandage wrapper in the trash and closed the first aid kit. "This is the house I told you about. The one my grandma bought."

Her jaw trembled, so she pressed her teeth together.

"This is the house *I* bought. Or rather, the one I was going to buy until you swept it out from under me."

His eyes widened, and his brow shot toward his hairline. "Oh, man. You have to believe I had no idea."

He seemed sincere, and his expression took the edge off her anger, but damn. This was *so* not how she expected this escapade to go. "Tell me what happened then."

He lifted his hands in a show of innocence. "I promise you I didn't know we were talking about the same house. My grandma has been dying to get her hands on this place for decades. The owner flat-out refused to sell, turned down every exorbitant offer she made. The only reason she was able to get it now was because he passed away and his estate sold it off."

"Well, I have been dying to get my hands on this place too, Eric." She shook her head, still trying to wrap her mind around it all. "Maybe not for decades, but from the moment Madeline showed it to me."

"I'm so sorry." He moved toward her, and she took a step back.

"I can't believe this. I was finally getting my life together. This place was…"

He dropped his arms by his sides. "What do you want me to do?"

"Sell it to me."

"I can't do that."

"Why not?"

"Well, for one, it's not mine. Grandma Landry owns it, and it's a family property. It belonged to my great-great-granddad's brother. He was moving to Mississippi for work, so my great-great-granddad bought it from him. He was going to give it to his daughter as a wedding gift."

His knowledge of the house's history dissolved what

was left of her anger. When she made the offer on the place, she hadn't looked into the history at all. The seller had disclosed a murder that happened in the eighties, but otherwise, Trish hadn't asked any questions because she was only thinking about the future of the house. The past hadn't crossed her mind, and that was a shame.

Every building in New Orleans had history. Not only was the city a living, breathing entity, but the homes were as well. She knew that, but in typical Trish fashion, she'd jumped at the chance to buy it without knowing anything about it.

She inclined her chin. "I suppose she never got the gift?"

Eric shrugged. "He was a compulsive gambler, lost it to his business rival in a poker game. It's been in their family ever since, and it ate away at my grandma to see it empty for so long."

"I see." She folded her arms across her stomach and gazed at the wall behind him. The home belonged with his family. That was better than a rich prick using it as a trophy mansion.

It still sucked royally, but she couldn't argue with history. The house had finally returned to its rightful owner. "What are you going to do with all the bedrooms?"

He leaned against the counter, crossing one ankle over the other. "I'll be living in one. As for the rest, I'm not sure. Grandma didn't mention wanting to do anything with them, so they'll probably be prop storage for the show, maybe an office."

Storage. What a waste of space.

A thud, followed by a scraping like furniture being dragged, sounded from upstairs, and Trish jerked her gaze to the ceiling. "You've already got people working on the house?" She hadn't even begun to look for a contractor. Truth be told, she hadn't done much of anything besides make an offer and imagine how grand the place would be when she was finished with it.

"No, I think we've got ghosts." His smile was an olive branch she needed to accept, so she grinned in return.

"Want to check it out?" he asked.

Oh, boy. "No thanks. Ghost hunting isn't my department." She needed to get home to her wine and cheese and sort through her emotions.

"C'mon. Don't make me confront the spirits by myself." He winked, and the corners of his eyes crinkled slightly with his smile, which made warmth spread through her chest.

How did he dissolve all her frustration with the simple closing of an eyelid? It had to be his psychic ability. His story that some people could block him from sensing their emotions was bunk. He always knew what to say to make her feel better. "Don't tell me the big, bad ghost hunter is scared."

"It'll be a lot less scary if I have a strong woman backing me up."

She rolled her eyes and laughed. "You're so full of shit."

"I'm not denying that. Come on." He gestured toward the stairs.

"All right, but then I need to go home and lick my wounds. This is the first time I've ever lost to you."

He froze on the bottom step and whirled around. "That's not true. What about at paintball?"

"You have *never* beat me at paintball."

He opened his mouth with a retort, but she cut him off. "Or laser tag, or Jenga." The Ghost Tours crew had a monthly game night, and Trish joined them every now and then.

He pursed his lips, narrowing his eyes. "We need to play more."

"Next time the crew gets together, I'm there."

"I'm looking forward to it."

She followed him to the second floor. Honestly, she was looking forward to it too. She enjoyed Eric's company way more than she should have. "I'm sorry for peeking in your window. I don't know what I was thinking."

He stopped on the landing and turned to her, taking both her hands in his. "And I am truly sorry about the house. If I hear of another one going up for sale, I'll let you know the moment it lists."

His hands were warm, his eyes sincere, and the spark she always felt around him flared back to life. But Eric was one mistake she'd managed to avoid for years, and she wasn't about to give in now. She cleared her throat and tugged from his grasp. "Thanks, but I've got Madeline on it. She'll probably know before you do."

"Please tell me I'm forgiven."

She shrugged, gave her eyes another roll, and shook her head. "You're forgiven. I can't really be mad after that story."

"Good." He grinned. "I think I heard the noise from this room." He stepped across the threshold, leaving Trish alone in the hallway. So much for needing a strong woman to have his back.

"Look at this." Excitement tinged his voice, and as she entered the room, he gestured to a massive armoire. "Scratch marks on the floor. This must have been what we heard."

Trish looked at the hardwood, and there were indeed

scratches where the legs met the floor. *Jeez. That's unsettling.* "Looks like you need to get the team out before the ghosts tear up the place."

Eric kneeled, ran his hand across the marred surface, and then rose to his feet. "You've got my attention," he said into the room. "Next time find a less destructive method if you want to talk."

Silence was the only response.

His excitement was contagious, and she found herself wishing he'd break out the ghost hunting equipment and show her how to use it. Even though Emily and Sean were both mediums and the whole team got together once a month at a haunted location, Trish had never been on an investigation. Sure, she found the spirit world fascinating, but after what happened to Emily, she left the ghost hunting to the professionals.

"Do you feel anything?" she asked.

He closed his eyes and inhaled deeply. His brow furrowed in concentration, and his chest rose and fell three times before he opened his eyes. "Nothing. Whoever did this isn't coming through."

"What do you feel from me?"

His grin returned. "What do you want me to feel?"

She crossed her arms and tried not to think about all the things she'd like to make *him* feel.

"I told you I don't have access to your emotions. You don't believe me?"

"Not really. No." She moved toward the door, making her escape before she said something she shouldn't. Being alone with Eric was way too tempting, despite her disappointment in the situation. "I'm going to leave you to it. I've got laundry waiting for me at home."

"Have you had dinner?" He followed her into the hall.

"That's waiting for me at home too."

"Let me take you out. We'll call it an apology dinner and then see where it goes."

Oh, I know exactly where it would go. "I'll see you around." She turned on her heel and darted down the steps before she could change her mind.

CHAPTER FOUR

"Good grief, this thing is heavy. Help me push it back into place." Eric leaned his back against the armoire, and Jason shoved with his shoulder. The sound of wood scraping wood made his skin crawl. He was certain these were the original floors, and his grandma would have a fit if they were ruined.

"You've got a strong one." Jason ran a hand through his dirty blond hair. "It took two grown men to move this sucker. Well, one grown and one half-grown."

"Shut up, man. I get enough of that from Trish." Eric could feel the teasing gesture came from a place of love. Jason—and the entire Ghost Tours team—loved to poke fun at each other, but the jokes about his age and maturity hit a sore spot.

"Sensitive much?" Jason followed Eric down the back staircase and into the kitchen. "Whatever happened with her? Last I heard, she bought you a drink and shot you down for the thirtieth time."

"A lot happened." He grabbed a bottle of Jameson and two glasses. "Drink?"

"Sure." Jason sank into a chair while Eric poured the whiskey.

A week had passed since he caught Trish sneaking around the place, and he hadn't heard hide nor hair from her. Not that he expected to. Their dynamic was reserved for group outings only, and the fact he'd seen her twice without her friends around was a miracle.

He sat at the table and slid a glass to Jason before taking a sip. "She was trying to buy this house."

Jason sputtered whiskey down his chin before wiping it away with the back of his hand. "This house? Really?"

He nodded. "She wanted to turn it into a bed and breakfast. Apparently, the seller had accepted her offer before my grandma bought it out from under her."

"Ouch. Looks like any chance you had with Trish has flown out the window."

"Tell me about it." He tossed back the rest of his drink and focused on the burn sliding down his throat, which was much more pleasant than the guilt churning in his gut. He wanted to make it up to her, but he had no idea how.

"Don't feel too bad. You know what would happen if you hooked up with her anyway."

He arched a brow. "Do I?"

Jason laughed. "The same thing that happens with every girl you date. You'll stick around for a few weeks and then leave her. You've got commitment issues. Best not to get involved with a woman you'll be seeing frequently for the foreseeable future."

It wasn't that he had commitment issues. The problem lay in his psychic ability. He could feel the emotions of the women he dated, and it was obvious when they were thinking about ending the relationship. So, he ended them first. All of them.

"Trish is different," he grumbled.

"Because she's hard—no, impossible—to get. You can't use your magic power to figure her out. You have to admit you love the chase."

Eric huffed. His friend had a point. He'd never met a woman he couldn't figure out. Not one he was attracted to anyway. Maybe his feelings for Trish were merely the childish obsession of wanting what he couldn't have. She seemed to think so, but...

"I don't know, man. I've never felt a spark like this about anyone, and it's lasted three years. I think it's more than the chase. I just wish there was something I could do to prove to her my feelings are real."

"Some kind of grand gesture, huh?" Jason screwed his mouth to the side and stared into his glass. "I got nothing. Sorry."

The front door opened, and Grandma Landry called, "Eric? I'm here for an update."

"Short of selling her this house, I don't either." He turned toward the foyer and shouted, "In the kitchen, Grandma."

They both stood as she entered the room, and Jason gave her a hug. "Hey, Mrs. Landry. It's good to see you."

She wore pale green pants with a cream silk shirt, and her light blonde hair was swept back in her signature twist. The wrinkles around her eyes deepened as she smiled and patted Jason's cheek. "You get cuter every day. Do you have a girlfriend yet?"

He chuckled. "No, ma'am. Not yet."

"My friend Margaret has an adorable granddaughter I could set you up with."

"If she's adorable, why don't you set Eric up with her?"

She blew a hard breath through her nose. "I tried. He refused." She shuffled toward Eric and hugged him before sinking into a chair. "Get your grandma a drink, will you?"

Eric smiled. "Sure thing." He grabbed another glass and poured the whiskey before setting it in front of her.

"What's this I hear about you wanting to sell this house? You know how hard I've fought for it."

For an old lady, she had damn good ears. "I wouldn't do that to you. Besides, your name is on the deed."

"And don't you forget it." She winked and sipped her drink. "Who were you talking about?"

Eric cut his gaze to Jason, who suppressed a smile. "Trish Bennett. You met her at Sydney and Blake's wedding."

She nodded thoughtfully. "Oh, yes. You've mentioned her quite a few times. She's a beautiful woman. I'm surprised you haven't asked her out yet."

"He has." Jason laughed. "Many times."

Eric shot him a look. "She thinks I'm too young."

"Nonsense." She waved off his statement. "Your grandfather was four years younger than me, and it didn't make a lick of difference. Maybe you should remind her that with youth comes more stamina in the bedroom. Your grandfather was a beast."

Eric closed his eyes for a long blink, willing the image from his mind. "TMI, Grandma."

She shrugged. "So Trish wants to buy this house?"

"She did buy it. Apparently, you bought it out from under her. You didn't tell me that."

Her mouth dropped open. "I didn't know."

Normally, Eric kept his ability in check around his

friends and family. They didn't appreciate him prying, but he let his shield slip slightly, and sure enough, surprise emanated from her aura.

"She wanted to run it as a bed and breakfast."

A sly smile curved her lips as she glanced at Jason and then Eric. "I think that's a fabulous idea."

He blinked. "What do you mean?"

"You're only planning to use the ballroom for your shows. You don't even need the kitchen since you're having the dinners catered."

"It would be a shame to let all this space go to waste." Jason grinned. "Wouldn't it, Mrs. Landry?"

"Indeed, it would, Jason. Eric, dear, why don't you call the contractor and have them add a few bathrooms upstairs? It'll take some space away from the rooms, but guests would rather a smaller bedroom with an ensuite bath than to share with a stranger. Landry House B and B will become a chain."

Eric gaped at his grandma. "Are you serious? You want me to offer Trish a job?"

"Not just any job. She'll be the lady of the house. I don't have time to run it, so all the management decisions will be up to her. I'll have a contract drawn up this afternoon."

Eric shook his head, still unbelieving. "You hardly know her."

"But you do. If you trust that she could run it, so do I."

Trish was confident and more than capable, but... "You can't make a snap decision like this."

"Who says it's snap?" She arched a brow. "I've been considering a second house for a while now."

"This might be that grand gesture that will show her your feelings are real," Jason said.

"She'll be over the moon." Grandma patted his knee. "All the perks of owning her own place without the mortgage payments. I'll take a percentage of her profits for rent, of course, but not much since she's your friend."

"I don't…" He stood and paced to the counter to pour another drink. "She wanted to live here. I doubt she'll want to move in with me. She won't even have dinner with me."

"The apartment above the garage is in decent shape. Have the contractors start the renovations there, and she can move in as soon as it's ready."

He sipped the whiskey, a mix of excitement and hesitation churning in his stomach, making his pulse race. "You realize this idea is insane, right? What if we make all these changes and she says no?"

"Then I'll find someone else to run it."

"Grandma…" She couldn't be serious. Not that Eric would mind the rooms being rented out. He grew up at Landry House, so he was used to guests.

"I've made my decision. Now, do I have to call the contractors, or will you do it?"

He let out a slow breath. The idea of seeing Trish every day both thrilled him and made him sick. So many things could go wrong with this setup…but what if things went right? "I'll do it."

"Good." She rose to her feet. "Show me the new plans as soon as they're drawn up."

As they walked Grandma Landry down the hall, a loud thud, followed by the same dragging sound Eric had heard a week ago, resonated from above.

"What on earth was that?" she asked.

"Our resident ghost, and you're not going to like what he's doing to the floor."

She gave Eric a sideways glance before climbing the stairs. He and Jason followed, and they found the armoire moved again, farther down the wall than the first time.

Grandma gasped. "These floors are original to the house. How dare you?" She glanced around the room as if waiting for the spirit to respond.

"I'm going to get the team out soon to see if we can get him to stop."

"Hey, Eric?" Jason called from the other side of the armoire. "I think the ghost might be trying to show you something."

He stepped around his grandma, and she licked her thumb and kneeled to try and rub the scratches out of the floor. What was it with old ladies thinking their spit was a cure for everything?

"Look." Jason slid his arm behind the armoire. "There's a seam here. It might be a door."

"Really?" Eric felt along the wall and found the break in the wallpaper. "Help me shove it aside. Watch out, Grandma."

"Wait!" She shot to her feet. "Put a drop cloth under it so it doesn't scratch the floor anymore." She grabbed a sheet that had covered the dresser.

Eric and Jason squatted, sliding their hands beneath the wood and lifting while Grandma placed one end of the drop cloth beneath the legs. The damn thing was so heavy, he nearly threw his back out raising it two inches from the floor. They did the same to the other side, and then all three pushed the armoire away from the wall.

"Holy crap. It is a door," Eric said.

"Language, young man," his grandma scolded.

"Sorry." Three locks lined the left side of the door, and he disengaged the first two before Jason grabbed his arm.

"Hold on. We have no idea what's locked in there."

"The house has been vacant for forty years. If anything is in there, it's dead."

"Exactly. We should wait for Sean and Emily."

Eric turned to his grandma, who had stepped away from the wall. A solemn look drew her features downward, and she clasped her hands together. "Open it."

Jason shook his head.

"It's her house." Eric threw open the last lock and tugged on the door. The musty stench of mold and decades of dust wafted out, and a wave of sadness slammed into him, nearly knocking him back.

"What's in there?" Jason stood behind him, looking over his shoulder.

A ray of sunlight slashed through the darkness from the tiny window on the far wall, but it wasn't enough to illuminate the whole room. Eric felt along the wall for a light switch, but he didn't find one so he turned on his phone's flashlight and stepped inside. Jason and Grandma followed, though she hovered in the doorway.

A twin-sized bed covered in an antique quilt lined one wall, and a small wooden chair with a matching table sat across from it. Otherwise, the room was bare. No wallpaper, no paint, no finish on the floor. He crept toward the bed and found leather shackles attached to all four posts. A chill crawled up his spine. "What is this place?"

"It's called a 'disappointments room.'"

He swung the light around to see his grandma, and she squinted. He switched the flashlight off, his eyes finally adjusting to the darkness. "What's that?"

"It's a secret room inside a house where the men would

lock away any family members who disappointed them." She stepped backward, out of the room.

Eric looked at Jason, who shrugged, and they followed her into the bedroom. "What does that mean?"

She sighed heavily. "Nowadays, people with mental illness can get help. They're treated like the human beings they are. When this house was built, it wasn't that way. If a man accused his wife of hysteria or one of his children didn't live up to his expectations, he could lock them up and hide them from society."

"That's horrible." He couldn't imagine such barbarism. Hell, with his ability and the way he freaked people when he was a kid, he probably would have been locked away back then. His mom, no doubt, would have been.

"It's an atrocity and a stain on the family name. You will have the contractors seal it up, and we'll never speak of it again."

"Seal it up? But it's part of the house, part of our history."

She inclined her chin. "Some history should be forgotten."

"But the people who suffered here shouldn't be."

"Seal it up." She gave him a pointed look that meant the conversation was over.

"Yes, ma'am."

"I want this armoire removed as well." She patted the hunk of furniture and left the room. "I'll send over the contract for Trish tomorrow," she called as she descended the stairs.

Eric returned to the disappointments room and let down his shields. So much pain and suffering happened in this space, he could hardly bear it. And the fact he could feel it at all meant spirits lingered, still in anguish.

"You okay?" Jason rested a hand on his shoulder, and he reeled in his ability.

"Yeah. Those locks are from the twentieth century. It wasn't just my family who used this room."

"Do you think it had something to do with the murder-suicide? Maybe the women were locked in here, and that was their only way of escape." According to the papers, a mother had murdered her daughter before killing herself in the 1980s. The father had moved out shortly after, and the house had sat vacant ever since.

"I don't know. I'll have to do some digging to find out."

"Are you really going to seal it up?"

He looked at the bed and the shackles. "Not yet." Not until he figured out exactly what had happened.

CHAPTER FIVE

"Any luck finding an apartment?" Emily leaned on the checkout counter as Trish shut down her workstation at the clinic.

"Nothing comparable to the one I'm about to leave. If I want a place that nice for the same price, I'm going to have to move farther out of the city. I am not looking forward to a longer commute." She slung her purse over her shoulder and stepped into the hallway.

"You know you're welcome to stay with us until you find something."

"Thanks. I appreciate that, but I need to do this on my own." She had to prove to herself she could make it despite her snap decision to buy a house and change careers falling apart. She could practically hear her step-mother's *I told you so* grating in her ears, and she wasn't about to let that woman be right. "Adrienne would be gloating right now if she knew I'd made yet another mistake."

"You didn't make a mistake. Sometimes things work

out as planned, and sometimes they don't. You couldn't have known."

"Things *never* work out as I plan."

"But you always *make* it work." Emily tilted her head. "Your dad had faith in you."

"He spoiled me."

"He gave you everything you needed, but he also taught you to be strong. Don't forget about how much you've accomplished since you got here. You're not married to the asshole you followed, and you're a better woman for it. You've got this."

"Thanks, Em." She shrugged. It was true her dad had faith in her. He told her he expected great things from her so many times; she couldn't bear to let him down now. She would be successful if it killed her.

Emily gave her a look of pity, which made her skin crawl. "Nothing from Madeline on the Tremé house?"

"It was way too small." She closed the office door. "Honestly, after almost owning Eric's gorgeous mansion, it's going to be hard to find something that intrigues me." Her heart sank at the mention of his name. She hadn't seen him in two weeks.

"That's understandable. Have you talked to him since?"

"No, I don't know what I would say. One on one conversations aren't our strong suit." Mostly because she had to stop herself from trying to jump his bones every time she saw him. It should be illegal for one man to possess that much sex appeal.

The door chimed, and a woman with a red nose and puffy eyes entered the clinic. She covered her mouth as she let out a hacking cough, and Trish cringed. "Have fun with that. What time is dinner Friday?"

"Seven o'clock."

"I'll be there." She gave her friend a quick hug and slipped into the lobby while the woman checked in. Emily must've had one hell of an immune system to deal with sick people face to face all day. At least Trish had the desk and a pane of plexiglass separating her from all the illness.

She pushed her shoulder against the door to shove it open and checked her phone for any messages from Madeline. Surely the "best real estate agent in New Orleans" could at least find her a nice apartment to rent within her budget. Sadly, she didn't have a single notification, so she made her way to the parking lot.

"Hey, Trish," the deep voice drew her attention, and she looked up to find Eric leaning against a silver Mazda. The same car she'd seen in the driveway of her...his... mansion two weeks ago. He used to drive a Toyota, which explained why she didn't recognize it before.

A flutter formed in her belly like it always did when she saw him. Hey, he was hot as sin. Any woman in her right mind would find him attractive. He wore dark jeans and a pale green button-up that brought out the emerald flecks in his hazel eyes, and he grinned when he caught her gaze.

She set her jaw. No matter how hot a fire he lit inside her, she would not succumb to his charm. Eric had a reputation, and Trish had no interest in being his latest conquest. Her career change may have been put on hold, but she refused to compromise on her list of requirements for a man. It was true love or no love, and based on the frequency Eric changed girlfriends, the real deal wasn't even on his radar. "When did you get a new car?"

He grabbed a backpack from the hood and stepped toward her. "A couple of months ago. How's it going?"

"Umm...fine. What are you doing here?"

"I was hoping to take you to lunch."

The flutter rose to her chest, but she shoved it down, her answer coming automatically, like it had the countless times he'd asked her out before. "Not a chance. How did you even know where I was?"

"I got Sean to ask Emily about your schedule." He drew his shoulders toward his ears, and for the first time since she'd known him, he looked almost nervous.

"That's..." She was going to say creepy, but the fact he'd gone to that much trouble to find her made her lips curve upward against her will. He always did this—disarmed her, made her feel better...special...even when she didn't want to.

"So Emily knew you'd be here?" She'd have to have words with her BFF if that were the case. They were supposed to tell each other everything.

"I don't think so. I asked Sean to do it without letting her know."

"Well, I'm sorry you wasted your time." She stepped back, clutching her purse strap on her shoulder. "I'll see you at the next group event."

"Just sit and talk with me over a meal. That's all I'm asking."

"Eric..." She shook her head. "You're ruining our dynamic. We don't see each other one on one."

"But listen."

"No." She strode toward her car. She was far too attracted to him to be having this conversation. Not only was he way too young and too nomadic with women, but if she did start dating him, she'd have to see him in her dream mansion and be constantly reminded of how she'd screwed up her life yet again. It would never work.

She hit the key fob to unlock her door. "We flirt, and then we part ways. We don't date."

"I'm not asking you on a date. I want to talk business."

"Business?" She opened the door.

"Trish, wait." He palmed it, slamming it shut. "I think you'll be interested in what I have to say."

Her mouth hung open at his boldness. Who did he think he was, trying to hold her hostage in the parking lot? And why did it turn her on? *Ugh! Get over yourself.* "What kind of business could you possibly want to discuss?"

"It's about the house." He squared his shoulders toward her. With his hand still on the car, he stood so close she could smell his warm, inviting scent, and man, oh man, did he smell good. Pheromone-revving, panty-dropping good.

Focus, Trish. Do not succumb to his masculine wiles. She lifted her hands and dropped them at her sides. "There's nothing to discuss. It belongs in your family."

"Please hear me out."

She sighed heavily. "If it will get you to leave me alone, fine. I'm listening."

"Let's go somewhere."

"It's two in the afternoon. I already ate lunch."

"Let's have coffee, then." He removed his hand from the car door and held both up in a show of innocence. "It's not a date."

Not a date, my ass. But an extra shot of caffeine wouldn't hurt. Plus, it was sweltering outside. The heat rose from the asphalt in visible waves, and her skin was in that clammy, right-before-the-sweat-starts-pouring phase.

It was a flimsy excuse for what she was about to do, but it was all she could come up with. And no, she was not giving in to his wiles. She was thirsty, damn it. "All right. There's a café a block over. I'll have an iced white mocha, and you're buying."

His cocky, lopsided grin affected her pulse in a way it shouldn't have. "I thought this wasn't a date."

"It's not." She strutted onto the sidewalk.

———

Eric jogged to catch up. Trish was still on the defensive when it came to being alone with him, but what he was about to offer her would be a game-changer...he hoped. Maybe.

He shoved his hands into his pockets and walked silently by her side as they crossed the street and entered the café. A counter stood at the back of the room, and six wooden tables filled the rest of the small space. Trish sank into a chair and crossed her legs. Her blonde hair caught the sunlight filtering through the window, and her pink lips formed an almost perfect bow.

He sauntered to the counter and ordered her mocha along with an iced latté for himself. He considered getting a plate of beignets, but that would be pushing it. He was lucky he got her to come for coffee.

Drinks in hand, he made his way to the table and sank into a chair before setting the plastic cup in front of her. "Iced white mocha, as requested."

She sniffed and grabbed the cup. "Thank you."

"This isn't so bad, is it? Two friends having a drink, discussing a business proposition." He held her gaze and sipped his latté. The milk tamed the bitterness of the espresso perfectly.

"I'll let you know once I hear what you have to say." Though she tried to hide it, she flashed a small smile.

Sometimes he wished he could sense Trish's emotions like he could with so many others, but it was a relief to feel normal with someone. They had a level playing field, which made her all the more intriguing. "First, I want to tell you that my grandma didn't know the seller had accepted your offer. They never mentioned it to her."

She lifted one shoulder. "It's fine."

"It's not fine, Trish. I feel horrible. And when I told her about your plans for the house, she made an offer I think you're going to like."

She pressed the straw to her lips and took a sip before setting the cup on the table and folding her hands. "I'm listening."

His nerves tied his stomach into knots. He still wasn't convinced this was a good idea, and he didn't know which would be worse: her accepting the deal and moving into the house or her shooting him down yet again.

"My grandma...we...want you to run the house."

She narrowed her eyes skeptically. "What do you mean 'run the house?'"

"She liked your idea of using the space as a bed and breakfast, and she wants you to be in charge of it. To be the 'lady of the house,' as she called it."

Her brows crept toward her hairline as she rested her forearms on the table. "A lady of the house *lives* in the house."

"You can pick any room you want and rent out the rest."

She laughed and leaned back in her seat. "I am not moving in with you, Eric. Nice try."

"I'll be staying in the apartment above the garage. The contractors are almost done with the renovations on that part."

"You…" She clutched her drink, her mouth working like she couldn't choose the right words. "I…"

"I won't get in your way. You'll hardly see me…unless you want to." He winked, trying to maintain their playful dynamic. It didn't work.

"You want me to be an *employee* in the house I was supposed to buy? Are you kidding?"

"Not an employee. The business will be entirely yours. You'll make all the decisions. The only difference from your original plan is that my grandma owns the house."

"So I'd be a tenant." Her expression was incredulous, and he didn't need his psychic ability to see she was less than impressed with his offer.

"Plenty of businesses rent the buildings they operate out of." He pulled the contract out of his bag and laid it on the table. "She wants a small percentage of your profits in return for using the space. That's it. The rest is up to you."

"I don't…" She huffed and shook her head. "This isn't my dream. I want to run *my own* business, not someone else's."

He pushed the contract toward her. "Read it. The business will be entirely yours. Sort of like a franchise. Everything you purchase for the B and B is yours to take with you whenever you decide to leave."

She crossed her arms and eyed the top page. "And you're okay with this? Where will you store all your props?"

"There's plenty of room in the garage."

"What if I need the space for storage?"

"I'm sure we can work something out. The place is huge." He held his breath, the answer to his previous dilemma becoming obvious: Trish rejecting the proposition would be *way* worse than her saying yes.

She chewed her bottom lip as she wiped the condensation from her cup. "Wouldn't you rather I say no so you can have the house to yourself?"

"If you say no, she'll find someone else to run it. Once Grandma Landry makes up her mind about something, there's no stopping her. I can't think of anyone I'd rather share the space with."

She flicked her gaze to meet his. "I don't know. It sounds like neither one of our dreams is coming true with this agreement."

"I see it as a way for both to come true…maybe even better than we dreamed." *Please say yes.*

She looked at her cup. "I'll have to think about it."

"The percentage she'll take is much less than a mortgage payment would be. Think of all the money you'll be saving."

"I said I'll think about it," she whispered before clearing her throat. "Thank you for the drink, but I've got to get home."

Eric rose as Trish did, and he took the contract from the table, offering it to her. "Read it over. My number is here when you're ready to talk about it." He pointed to the top right portion of the page.

Trish nodded, took the stack of papers, and hurried out the door.

CHAPTER SIX

*E*ric forced himself to walk slowly so his tour group could keep up. Sweltering summer air clung to his skin, and the ice in his water bottle had long since melted. He adjusted his shirt as a bead of sweat rolled down the middle of his back, but the heat wasn't what had him anxious for this tour to end.

An email from the parish archives had pinged his phone at the start of the excursion, and he was dying to see the contents. But first, he had to deliver his speech about the most notorious house in New Orleans. He side-stepped around a couple arguing on the sidewalk and crossed the street to stand in front of a dark gray neoclassical mansion on Royal Street.

"Welcome to the most haunted house in the French Quarter, the LaLaurie Mansion." He gestured to the house with a flourish. "Who here has heard of it?"

A woman with long brown hair stepped forward. "Wasn't this place on *American Horror Story*?"

"It was, but before you get too excited, most of the filming was done in a house on St. Louise Street."

"Can we go inside? Do they do tours?" a man asked.

Eric shook his head. "It's a private residence now, but it has been an apartment complex and an all-girls school since the ghastly happenings of the 1830s."

He paused for dramatic effect, and his group drifted closer, hanging on his word. "Madame Delphine LaLaurie was the lady of the house, and she was known for throwing lavish parties with her third husband. I should mention her first two husbands died under mysterious circumstances." Another pause to heighten the suspense.

"So she killed number three?" a woman in her fifties with curly hair and bright red nails asked.

Eric chuckled. "Why do you sound excited about the idea?" He winked, and her smile widened. "Sorry to disappoint, but she did not kill husband number three. But if you believe the rumors, she may have killed many, many others."

He wove the tale of a fire breaking out in the kitchen, and when the firefighters arrived, they found an enslaved person chained to the stove. Apparently, Madame LaLaurie had done some appalling things to the rest of the people she'd enslaved. So appalling, in fact, that the residents of New Orleans busted in, ransacked the house, and nearly destroyed it.

Of course, only one newspaper at the time reported on the atrocity, and they later stated it was a smear campaign instigated by a disgruntled neighbor. But the tourists hardly listened to that part. They always preferred to hear about the gory lore.

"Supposedly, the mansion is cursed, and Delphine went mad because of it."

"Is it really?" the brunette asked.

Eric shrugged. "Depends on whom you ask and

whether or not you believe in curses. I will say that, since the LaLauries, no one has lived in this house longer than five years, and many of them wound up in financial ruin."

Gasps emanated from his audience, followed by whispers as they discussed the curse with their friends.

"Nicholas Cage owned this house for a hot minute back in 2009. He filed for bankruptcy and lost it shortly after he bought it, so believe what you will."

"Who owns it now?" The brunette had made her way to the front of the group, and Eric sucked in a deep breath, making sure his ability was in check. He could tell from her body language she was interested in more than the tour.

He cleared his throat and stepped off the curb between two parked cars. "I hear it's an oil tycoon from Texas. He doesn't live there, so he's breaking the ownership record."

"Smart man," she said.

"This concludes the guided part of our tour, folks. Your ticket also includes entrance to the Museum of the Macabre, which is just a few blocks away. It's open until ten tonight, but you're welcome to visit anytime during your stay."

Eric bowed, and several people in his group clapped. "If you enjoyed yourselves, my name is Eric. Please leave us a review on Yelp or Trip Advisor. If you didn't, well, you keep that to yourself if you don't mind."

His audience laughed, and several slipped him tips when they shook his hand. He said goodbye to the last one and turned to go, but the brunette blocked his path.

"That had to be the most entertaining tour I've ever been on." She cut her gaze across the street where her friend stood waiting for her.

"Thank you, ma'am. I appreciate that."

"Ma'am?" She laughed. "I'm not that much older than you, am I?"

"Most definitely not. You don't look a day over twenty-one."

"Good, because I'm twenty-three."

He switched off the iPad he'd used to show them examples of paranormal evidence and folded the cover over the front. "Well, have a nice night."

He strode past her, but she caught up and matched his pace. "It's a shame you don't have any evidence from inside the LaLaurie mansion. That would be cool."

"It sure would, but even tour guides aren't allowed inside. I've got to—"

"Do you ever do private tours?" She motioned for her friend to join them, and Eric let his shield slip. As expected, she didn't want a tour; she wanted a date.

He tensed. He normally would have jumped at the chance to spend the evening with two beautiful women. Tonight, and hell, every night for the past two and a half weeks, his mind was occupied with two things. Figuring out what happened in the mansion's disappointments room and Trish. Not necessarily in that order. He couldn't get the woman off his mind.

"I'm afraid I don't, and I'm running late meeting someone. Have a nice night, ladies." He strode away before they could respond.

As he reached the entrance to the museum, which also housed the Crescent City Ghost Tours headquarters, he spotted several people from his tour group standing outside. He ducked through the gate blocking the alley between buildings and entered the offices through the back door.

Blake, the museum's curator, sat in his office, and Eric

knocked on the open door. "Hey, man. Can I use your computer for a second? I need to see something on a big screen."

"Sure." He closed the program he was using and rose to his feet before gesturing to the chair.

"Thanks. Has Jason made it by yet?" Eric dropped into the seat and logged in to his email.

"I think he's in Sydney's office."

"Hey, Jason," Eric shouted toward the doorway. "Get your ass in here."

Footsteps sounded from the hall before Jason appeared in the threshold. "What's up, man? Good tour tonight?"

"Fantastic." He couldn't fight his grin. "The parish archives came through. I got the plans."

"Sweet! Pull them up." He moved to stand behind Eric.

"Are you boys planning something without me?" Sydney leaned a shoulder against the door jamb and crossed her arms. She wore Converse, ripped jeans, and a black tank that showed off her Alice in Wonderland tattoo sleeve.

"If they are, I'm clueless to what it is." Blake held out his arm, and Sydney moved to his side. "What are y'all talking about? Archives and plans?"

"It's here." Excitement made Eric's knee bounce beneath the desk as the original architectural plans for the mansion opened on his screen. "That was the third bedroom from the left, so it would be right here." He pointed to the spot on the floor plan.

"It's one big room." Jason leaned in closer, and Sydney and Blake crowded around the computer.

Eric's gaze darted over the plan, checking to see if he'd miscalculated the location of the disappointments room.

He'd found the right spot, and there was no trace of an extra room. "It extends all the way to the exterior wall, see? There's the little window."

"What are we looking for?" Blake asked.

Jason straightened. "Eric's house has a disappointments room."

Eric logged out of his email and rotated the chair to face his friends. "It's a secret room where the men could lock up the women and children who didn't live up to their expectations."

Sydney cringed. "I saw a movie about that once. It's such an awful thing."

"It is, but the room isn't on the original plans for the house. That means it was added later."

"Okay…" Blake furrowed his brow.

"That means my ancestors didn't have the room built. It's not a stain on my family's name after all."

"Eric's grandma wants the room sealed up and it never spoken of again," Jason said.

"But I think it needs to be explored. The people who suffered there need to be remembered. Now, she won't have an objection."

"Unless the room was so secret, your ancestor had it built but not included on the floor plan," Sydney said. "It could have been a verbal agreement between him and the builders."

"Crap." His shoulders slumped. "I didn't think about that."

"When's the contractor scheduled to start on that part of the house?" Jason asked.

"Next week." Eric looked at Blake. "The force of emotions that slammed into me when I opened the door was unbelievable. I've never felt anything from an inanimate object before, but for a second or two, that room felt alive. If that much spirit energy is lingering, I can only imagine what the walls have absorbed. Would you be interested in checking it out?"

Blake had psychometric abilities. He could read the energy attached to objects and put together a profile of the living who left their energy behind. "I'd love to."

Sydney rested her hand on Blake's chest. "As long as it isn't going to have a negative effect on him. Give me some time to meditate on it first, and then we'll let you know."

Sydney was clairvoyant, and while she couldn't always see someone's future, when she did, her visions were uncanny.

"Way to make a guy feel useless." Jason leaned on the edge of the desk. He was the only person in the Ghost Tours group who didn't have any sort of psychic ability. Well, Trish didn't either, but she didn't work for the company.

Eric clapped him on the shoulder. "You're far from useless. You found the room in the first place."

"That's true." He straightened his spine. "Hey, have you heard from Trish? Did she agree?"

"Not yet. It's been two days since I asked her, so I'm starting to doubt she will. She wasn't thrilled about the idea." He shook his head, the excitement over the floor-plans giving way to his disappointment. "I can't seem to do anything right when it comes to her."

Sydney gave him a sympathetic look. "Sometimes a person can't see a good thing when it's staring her right in the face. Don't give up yet."

He arched a brow. "Did you see something?"

She laughed. "No, and even if I did, you know it wouldn't matter. I see what will happen if things continue down the path they're on. Things can always change."

"It was worth a shot." He could use all the help he could get when it came to that woman. All he wanted was the chance to show her how perfect they were for each other, and if she would accept the offer and move into the mansion, he'd have loads of opportunities.

If she said no, well, he'd have to figure something else out.

Trish scooped up the last bite of her crawfish etouffee before wiping her mouth with a napkin. "You're so lucky being married to a man who likes to cook." Of course, if Trish were being served restaurant-quality Cajun food every night, she'd have to invest in a wardrobe of sweats and yoga pants.

Emily laughed. "And he makes sure I don't forget it."

"What can I say? I'm perfect." Sean winked at Emily, and she smiled in return.

"All right, love birds. Don't rub it in." Trish stood and carried her plate to the sink.

Emily and Sean had been adorable together from day one. He wasn't perfect, but they were perfect for each other. And while Trish was happy for her best friend, she couldn't help the twinge of envy tightening her stomach.

"I don't think I'll ever find what you two have. Especially not with the guys I've met on the dating apps." There had to be a good one out there somewhere; she simply hadn't found him yet. "Maybe my standards are too high."

A look passed between Emily and Sean before she

stood and said, "You brought the contract, right? Can I see it?"

"It's in my bag." Trish rinsed her plate while Sean cleared the rest of the dishes, and then she and Emily went to the living room.

She handed her friend the stack of papers and settled on the couch next to her. "I don't know, Em. It still feels like he's trying to hire me to be his employee. I don't want to work for Eric." There were plenty of other things she wanted to do with him, but those things would never happen.

"It didn't sound that way at all when you described it. Let me look it over, and I'll tell you what I think."

Trish sat silently as Emily scanned the documents. A toy shaped like a glow worm lay on the coffee table, and she picked it up, giving it a squeeze. The worm giggled, and music played from its belly.

Emily looked up from her reading. "Please don't wake up Sable. I just put her to bed before you got here."

"Sorry." She laid the toy on the table, and Sean sauntered into the room.

"How does it look?" He sank into a blue accent chair.

Emily handed him the contract. "I can't find any drawbacks. The only mention of Eric is that he gets to use the space downstairs in the main house for his murder mystery shows. He'll have nothing to do with the bed and breakfast."

Trish knew that already. She'd read the contract at least four times since he'd given it to her, and almost everything about it was positive. It should have been a no-brainer, but... "The drawback is he'll be there all the time. I'll probably see him every single day."

Emily suppressed a smile. "How awful it would be to

live on the same property with a man who would shower you with affection if you'd give him half a chance."

Trish crossed her arms. She'd thought about that too. "Maybe I don't want to be showered with affection."

Emily arched an eyebrow. "Okay, Miss Pants on Fire. What are you afraid of?"

"You know what. It's no secret I'm attracted to him. It's also no secret that he bounces from girlfriend to girlfriend like a dodge ball in a high school gym class. Suppose I do let him shower me with affection? What happens when he bounces from me? I'll be stuck in his house seeing him all the time while he moves on to his next target."

Sean flipped through the contract and pointed at a page. "According to this, you won't be stuck anywhere. You're free to leave at any time and take all the furnishings you purchased for the business with you. This is the most generous contract I've ever seen. If I were you, I'd close this deal before Mrs. Landry changes her mind."

"I'd still be practically living with a man I'm attracted to, whom I don't want to date." Why was it so hard for them to understand the issue?

"So don't date him." Emily shrugged like it was the most obvious solution in the world. "If you're dead set against having a relationship with Eric, then don't have one. Talk to him, tell him if it's going to work the most you can offer is friendship. I know you don't believe it, but he's a mature guy. I'm sure he'll accept your terms. If he doesn't, then *you* can bounce."

Huh. There was a thought. As she'd mulled over the idea in her mind for the past two days, all she'd considered was what would happen when one thing led to another.

But one thing didn't have to lead to anything. It would

take self-control on her part, but Eric was nothing if not respectful of women. If she stopped flirting, he would too.

"Eric is a standup guy," Sean said, almost as if reading her mind. "He's reliable, responsible, and loyal."

"Which are all good reasons to give him a chance, but what do I know about overlooking what you consider a fatal flaw?" Emily shrugged.

Trish gave her the stink eye. Her bestie could write the book on that subject.

"He hasn't found the right woman yet," Sean added. "When he does, he'll stick around."

"I am definitely not the right woman for someone so young."

"Okay, then there's your answer." Emily fought another smile. "You're not the right woman for him, so tell him that and actually *mean it*. You're too old for the game y'all have been playing anyway."

"You're right." Trish straightened her spine. "You're absolutely right. I'm a grown woman. I can spend time with an attractive man and not let it lead to anything. Why not?"

"I don't see how you can lose with this deal," Emily said.

"Sean, hand me the contract. I'm going to text Eric right now. I already lost the house once. I'm not going to lose it again."

Sean set the contract on the coffee table and slid it toward her as she tugged her phone from her pocket. She typed in Eric's number and sent him a message: *It's Trish. I'm ready to talk. When can we meet?*

"There." She set the phone on the table. "But I'm not going to stop looking for a house to buy. I'm going to use this opportunity to gain as much experience as possible.

Then, when I find my own mansion, I can hit the ground running."

"That sounds like an excellent plan," Emily said.

Her phone buzzed, and she swiped it open to read his response: *How about dinner tomorrow night?*

"That man does not know when to give up, does he? He wants to have dinner."

Sean chuckled. "Did I mention he's persistent and always goes after what he wants?"

"Two more good traits," Emily sang.

Trish ignored her and typed a reply: *Seven o'clock, and it's not a date. It's business.*

CHAPTER SEVEN

"How do I look?" Eric turned in a circle in his grandma's living room, showing her his choice in attire for his not-a-date with Trish. He'd opted for dark denim and a crisp, black button-up.

"Jeans, Eric?" She shook her head. "Don't you think slacks would be more appropriate for your first date?"

"It's not a date. Besides…" He sat on the edge of a nineteenth-century chaise lounge. "I don't want to look like I'm trying too hard."

She leaned back, taking in his clothes and pressing her lips together like she wanted to chide him. Thankfully, she refrained. "Where are you taking her?"

"Muriel's in Jackson Square."

She flicked her gaze to his eyes. "It's a date."

"It's not." He opened the message thread and showed it to her. "Read the last one."

She took her glasses from the end table and set them on her nose before peering at the screen. She studied it for a moment, handed it back to him, and folded her frames. "It's a date."

Eric laughed. "If you say so." Truth be told, with the way his nerves were reacting, it might as well have been a date. He'd already sweated through his first layer of deodorant and had to take a second shower. After some deep breathing and a ten-minute pep talk, he'd managed to calm himself down enough to stay dry. His grandma insisting it was a date wasn't helping.

"Anyway, I stopped by because I wanted to talk to you about the disappointments room."

The moment he uttered the last two words, her demeanor did a one-eighty. Her posture stiffened, and her mouth tightened at the corners. "There's nothing to talk about."

He scooted forward. "I did some research, and I got ahold of the original floor plans. It wasn't on them, so I don't think our family—"

"Eric," she snapped. "I told you I want that room sealed up. When is it scheduled to happen?"

He ground his teeth. Why was she being so stubborn about this? "Next week."

"I'll call the contractor tomorrow morning. I want it done by Sunday."

"Grandma, if you'll—"

"You don't want to be late for your first date with Trish. Run along now." She picked up a novel, ending the conversation.

He wanted to argue more, to find out why she reacted so strongly to the disappointments room. As far as he knew, she'd never set foot inside the house until it was sold, so she couldn't have any personal experience with it. Could she have known someone who was locked inside it? That was a possibility, but he didn't have time to find out. He had thirty minutes to make it to the French Quarter to meet Trish.

He parked at Ghost Tours HQ and walked to Jackson Square. A breeze rolled down St. Peter Street, providing a welcome reprieve from the summer heat, and the afternoon sun painted the clouds pink and orange. Creole cottages in pastel shades of yellow, blue, and pink lined either side of the street, their front windows shuttered to offer privacy from the prying eyes of passersby.

The quiet of the residential area gave way to music and chatter as he approached Bourbon Street. He sidestepped a group of men about his age, and the distinct scents of hurricanes and weed billowed around them. He picked up his pace the final few blocks, but the quickening of his pulse was due more to what was about to happen than to his increase in speed.

Though he arrived with two minutes to spare, Trish was already there, standing on the sidewalk outside Muriel's. She wore a short, emerald green dress that hugged her curves, and she'd pinned one side of her hair back with a matching jeweled clip.

She smiled as he approached, and as she swept her gaze down his form, she inhaled deeply as if she liked what she saw. "About time you got here."

"You look stunning." He stopped in front of her, fighting the urge to lean in and kiss her cheek. They weren't close enough for that kind of gesture yet.

"This…" She pressed her lips together, holding his gaze for a moment. "Thank you. You look nice as well."

"Shall we?" He opened the door and gestured for her to enter.

"Thanks." She stepped inside, and he followed.

The host guided them to a room with maroon walls

and thick, white crown molding. Tables draped in white stood on polished wood floors, and several crystal chandeliers filled the space with warm light.

Eric pulled out a cherry wood chair for Trish, and she accepted the gesture without protest this time. He took the seat across from her, and the host handed them the menus.

"This place is nice." Trish glanced around the room, looking at everything but him. "I've never been here before."

"The wood-grilled pork chop is delicious. The meat practically melts on your tongue."

She flicked her gaze to his, and heat sparked in her eyes before she cleared her throat and laid her menu on the table. "That sounds good. I'll have that."

"Me too." He waited for her gaze to meet his once more. "I know this isn't a date, but do you mind if I order a bottle of cabernet? It pairs nicely with the pork."

"Interesting." She tilted her head, looking thoughtful.

"What? You don't like red?"

"No, I do. I like all wines, except for ports and other really sweet ones. I'm surprised you like red."

"And why is that?"

"I waited tables at an Italian restaurant when I was young. As a general rule, people in their twenties drink rosé. In their thirties, they graduate to whites, and they don't like reds until they reach their forties."

"You like red, and you're only thirty."

She lifted one shoulder dismissively. "I'm an anomaly."

"So am I. Should I order it? We are celebrating, after all."

"What are we celebrating?" she asked in a playful tone.

"You're finally getting to run your own B and B."

She clamped her mouth shut, her eyes tightening as she studied him. She inhaled as if she were about to speak, but the server arrived and filled their glasses with water. She told them about the specials, and Eric ordered the bottle of wine.

"I'll have the pork chop." Trish handed the server the menu.

"I'll have the same." He waited for the woman to walk away before turning to Trish. "You don't normally carry a bag that big, so I assume you have the contract inside?"

Her hand dropped to the satchel hanging on the back of her chair. "I do, but we need to discuss a few things."

"Okay."

"First of all, why are you going to live in the garage apartment while I get to stay in the main house? The mansion belongs to your family. It seems like you're getting the short end with this setup."

"The original contract had you living in the apartment. I had my grandma change it."

"Why?"

He shrugged. "It makes more sense for you to live in the house since you'll be running it. Plus, that was your dream, right? To live in one room and rent out the rest?"

"Yes, it was…it is."

"There you go. I'm trying to make this as close to your dream setup as possible."

A look of surprise flashed across her features before she lowered her gaze and then looked into his eyes. "That's very kind of you."

"What can I say? I'm a nice guy." And he would do whatever it took to make Trish happy. "Anything else you want to discuss?"

She folded her hands in her lap. "Since the house

belongs to your grandma, I assume she'll be stopping by to check on things."

"Most likely, but she'll respect your privacy. She won't have a key to your living area, and she won't meddle in your business unless it's floundering. Landry House has a reputation to uphold."

"I understand that, but will any of your other relatives be dropping in? What part does your mom play in all of this? I know old money families like yours are tight, and I don't want to deal with drama."

He straightened his spine. "How do you know that?"

"Because my dad came from one. They never approved of my mom, and they were thrilled when she and my dad got divorced. The drama in that family was... I'm glad to be rid of it."

Interesting. That was the most she'd ever shared about herself with him. "My grandma raised me. I haven't seen my mother in more than a decade, so I doubt you'll have to worry about her."

She blinked, her brow lifting. "Oh. I didn't know. I'm sorry."

"Nothing to apologize for. The family drama ended when she gave me up."

She tilted her head, her expression softening. "What about your dad?"

"Never in the picture, and my grandpa passed away when I was a baby."

"Siblings?"

"Don't have any."

"Neither do I," she said softly.

"Look at that. We have something in common after all."

The server arrived to pour the wine, and Eric lifted his glass in a toast. "To making our dreams come true."

Trish clinked her glass to his, but her expression hardened. She set her wine on the table without taking a sip and folded her arms in front of her. "If I'm going to do this, we have to lay down some ground rules."

He swirled the wine in his glass and took a drink. "Okay, shoot."

She inhaled deeply and blew her breath out hard, nodding in resolve. "This flirting game that we have going on has to stop. You and I are never going to happen, so we can't keep pretending like we might."

Ouch. He forced a neutral expression, but damn. They weren't even a couple, so why did this feel like a breakup? Aside from his mother abandoning him, he'd never been dumped before. It wasn't a cool feeling. Not at all.

"We'll still be friends, of course," she said. "You're a great guy, but if we're going to be working so closely, we have to keep it professional. Friends only."

Yeah, this felt way too much like a breakup, and she sounded way too much like she meant it. Well, like she was trying to mean it.

He cleared his throat and pulled himself together, straightening his spine. "I agree. Games like that don't belong in the workplace, and obviously, it was never going to lead to anything more."

"Obviously," she agreed, though the look on her face was one of wariness. She had doubts about the arrangement she proposed, but he wasn't sure if it was *his* ability to be friends she questioned or hers.

"Okay, then." She lifted her glass toward him. "To friendship and making dreams come true."

"To friendship." He tapped his glass to hers, and this

time, she didn't just take a sip; she drained the whole thing.

Well, that was a disaster. Eric sat on a box in the living room, tapping his foot as he waited for Blake to arrive. He'd texted him as soon as his awkward dinner with Trish ended, and he'd agreed to come read the disappointments room tonight.

Okay, the whole dinner wasn't an awkward disaster. It started out great. Hell, he'd learned more about Trish in one evening than he had in the entire time he'd known her. But this just being friends business... He could do it outwardly, but it would slowly kill him on the inside.

A knock sounded, and he shot to his feet, paced to the foyer, and swung open the door. "Thanks for coming out on such short notice."

"No problem." Blake stepped inside and followed him to the staircase. "Your grandma is dead set against anybody knowing about this room, isn't she?"

"She refuses to talk about it. Anytime I try to get her to explain why, she clams up. She's got the contractors coming out tomorrow morning to seal it, so this is our only chance." He led the way up the steps.

"How did your dinner with Trish go?" Blake kept his hands in his pockets and turned in a circle on the landing, taking in the home.

Eric let out a dry laugh. He should've known the entire crew would hear about it. "Businesswise, it was great. She signed the contract, and she's moving in next week."

He arched a brow, silently urging him to continue.

"Then she said the 'flirting game' we've been playing has to end." He made air quotes. "She relegated me to the friend zone."

"Damn. I'm sorry, man. You okay?"

Eric shrugged. "It is what it is." He'd respect her wishes, but he refused to give up hope. The more he got to know her, the stronger his feelings for her became, and he could tell—even without his sixth sense—she felt more than friendship toward him. "This is the room." He gestured to the bedroom, and they stepped inside.

Blake let out a low whistle and strode to the door, his hands still tucked firmly into his pockets. "Somebody did not want the person they trapped in here getting out."

"I can't even imagine."

He removed his hands from his pockets and shook them before cracking his knuckles. "It'll take me a minute to piece it all together. I only get glimpses of the past when I do this."

"Take all the time you need."

Blake nodded and pressed his hands against the locks. Inhaling deeply, he closed his eyes. "I sense male energy. Several males from different time periods." He took a few more deep breaths. "It was definitely the men locking people up. I feel frustration and despair, but the shame overpowers it."

"That sounds about right. They locked up anyone in their family they were ashamed of back then."

"Some of the energy is more recent. The 1950s maybe."

"Really?" If that were the case, it wasn't just possible his grandma knew someone who was locked in here. It was probable. "What about inside?"

Blake crossed the threshold and stood in the center of

the room. Without speaking, he paced to the wall and placed both palms against it. Eric leaned in the door jamb, watching as he moved to the window, running his hands along the sill before resting them both on the back of the wooden chair.

"This is…" He shook his head. "This is bad."

"What happened in here?"

"Hold on." He moved to the bed, first laying his hands on the mattress and then on the posts and shackles. He visibly shuddered. "Okay. I need to step out."

He strode out the door and down the stairs without saying a word. When they reached the foyer, he finally spoke. "The people locked in the room were all women. All wives of the men who owned the house over the years. First wives, second wives."

Eric's mouth hung open, so he snapped it shut.

"I felt madness. The women were panicked, having fits of mania, and one kept saying, 'we're cursed.' Maybe mental illness ran in the family. Maybe the men drove the women crazy. I don't know, but I can understand why your grandma would want that room sealed up. Nothing but misery happened in there."

"The women married into the family, so it couldn't be a hereditary mental illness. Could it be possible that every man who owned this house drove his wife insane? How…?"

"A shared delusion?" Blake lifted his hands and dropped them at his sides. "I don't know that it was every woman, but the house stayed in the same family, right? Maybe fathers passed the delusion on to their sons."

"That's crazy."

"With that much suffering in one place, you must

have ghosts. Maybe a spirit was the cause. Maybe something darker."

A shiver ran up Eric's spine. "That would explain the murder-suicide that happened in the eighties. Emily is coming to help Trish unpack next week. She said she'd look for ghosts when she's here."

"Does Trish know about the disappointments room?"

"I haven't mentioned it."

"Considering she's a woman who's going to be living in a house where so many went insane, you probably ought to tell her."

"Yeah, I guess I probably should." Hopefully it wouldn't be a deal-breaker for her.

CHAPTER EIGHT

*T*rish set a moving box on her bed and wiped the sweat beading on her brow. She'd hired movers to bring over her mattress and the larger containers, but she'd also brought a few items here in her car.

The dark wood bed frame was absolutely gorgeous, with an intricately carved headboard that sported a fully bloomed rose as a centerpiece. Why the previous owners moved this nineteenth-century piece to a spare bedroom and opted for a particleboard-framed waterbed, she couldn't fathom. Then again, it was the eighties when they lived there.

"This is the last one from your backseat." Eric set a box on top of a stack behind her. "Do you have more in the trunk?"

"That's the last of them. Thanks for your help." She smiled, and he grinned in return, which made her pulse quicken.

"My pleasure." He pressed his lips together and tapped a finger against his thigh. "Are you one hundred percent sure you want to live here, knowing the history?"

She sighed. He'd called her last week with a sordid story about women being locked up in a secret room. "I told you on the phone nothing is going to stop me from doing this."

His brow furrowed. "Even though so many of them went mad?"

"They probably went mad *because* they were locked up. Men did terrible things to women back then." She crossed her arms. "And if it's the ghosts, Emily will be here any minute. She'll find them and figure out how to make them stop."

"What if there's something darker here?"

"Then we'll call Sydney's Voodoo priestess friend to get rid of it." She cocked her head. "It sounds like you're trying to get rid of me. Have you changed your mind about this setup?"

"Not at all. I just want to be sure you're safe."

Her chest tightened at the sincerity in his voice. Add sweet and protective to his list of positive traits. Damn. Being just friends was going to be harder than she thought. "I'm a big girl. I can take care of myself."

"I don't doubt that. You don't mind living here during the renovations? It'll be loud during the day."

"It was my plan to begin with. My lease is up, so I have to live somewhere. Better here than to move twice." She ripped the tape off the box. "Do you have any more reasons why I shouldn't want to be here? Do *you* not want me to be here?"

"I want you to be here." Heat sparked in his gaze, and if the game were still on, he probably would have followed with a list of all the places in the house he wanted her. But he was a good boy, and he left it at that, unfortunately.

No, not unfortunately. His compliance with her ground rules was a good thing.

She cleared her throat. "Where is this disappointments room?"

"It's sealed up." He gestured toward the hall, and she followed him to a bedroom three doors down. He paced across the room and ran his hand along a wall that didn't match the rest of the room. The drywall was smooth, and the paint looked brand new, while dark green paper covered the other three walls. "My grandma had the contractors stop what they were doing to close it off."

"Did you at least take pictures?"

"Of course." He pulled his phone from his pocket, and Trish stood next to him.

As he held the device out, flipping through the pictures and zooming in to show her the details, she drifted closer. His scent was warm and inviting, like a campfire on a winter night. He cleared his throat, and she realized she'd leaned so close her shoulder pressed against his.

She jerked away. "Can you send me those? I'd like to look at them closer."

"Sure thing."

She hurried out of the room and reminded herself to breathe. Eric did *not* tick all her boxes, and she refused to waste her time with anyone who couldn't offer the possibility of something long-term. But damn... The physical attraction... He didn't just tick that box; he filled the sucker in with a Sharpie.

As Eric entered the hall, a loud thud sounded from Trish's room. They paced to the doorway and found the box she'd opened on her bed lying on its side on the floor, the contents scattered about the room.

"Told you we've got ghosts." Eric kneeled and began picking up the spilled items.

"I probably left it too close to the edge." Trish flipped the box upright and gathered her alarm clock and flashlight, and *oh crap*, this box held the contents of her nightstand. "It's okay. I've got this." She scrambled to get the rest of her belongings.

Eric chuckled and laid a few things in the box, including a box of condoms *and* her hot pink vibrator. He pursed his lips, his brow raising like he wanted to say something he shouldn't. "I think I found what you're so desperately looking for."

Her cheeks burned, and fingers of heat lapped all the way to her ears. Not only did he see her sex toy, but he picked it up...touched it with his hands...and laid it gingerly in the box. *Oh, the humiliation.* Then again, the idea of using it when his hands had been on it did have a strange appeal. *What is wrong with me?*

"Thanks," she said curtly, and praise the doorbell gods, a deep, melodious chime sounded through the house. "That'll be Emily." She shot out of the room and descended the front staircase like the floor was on fire before swinging open the door. "Hey, Em. Come on in."

"This is so exciting." Emily stepped into the foyer and turned in a circle. "Wow. It's gorgeous in here."

"They started the renovations on the downstairs, and it's pretty much done. We're just waiting for the new cabinets in the kitchen. The upstairs will take a lot longer."

"When can you open up shop?"

"It'll be at least six months. I'm sure Eric will be able to start his business before I do. The ballroom is done except for the furniture and wall-hangings." She led her to the room Eric would be using for his shows. The dark wood floor had been refinished, and it shone in the sunlight streaming in through the windows. The contractor had built a small platform for Eric to stand on during his shows, and a door leading out to the garden would allow people to step outside during meals. The walls were bare, but Eric had assured her his family had plenty of paintings to decorate the space.

Emily nodded in appreciation. "This is so nice. Show me your room."

They headed for the staircase just as Eric was coming down. "Hey Eric," Emily said. "The house looks fantastic."

"Thanks. It's good to see you again." He glanced at Trish and suppressed a smile. "Are we doing ghosts first or unpacking?"

"Unpacking," Trish said, unable to meet his gaze.

"Well, I'll leave you ladies to it. Let me know if you need any help, and I'll be back when the fun starts." He turned and headed down the hallway to the back of the house.

"How's *that* going?" Emily raised a questioning brow.

"Oof. Come upstairs, and I'll tell you." She led the way to her new room and plopped onto the bed. "Close the door. He probably went back to his apartment, but I don't want to chance him overhearing."

Emily did as she was asked and then sank onto the bed next to Trish, folding one leg beneath her. "I know that look. Is he not honoring his end of the deal?"

"He touched my vibrator, Em. With his hands."

Emily's eyes widened, her brow creeping upward as she waited for Trish to say more. "Care to elaborate?"

"This box with all my nightstand stuff got knocked off the bed. He was helping me clean up the mess, and he picked up my vibrator and a pack of condoms like it was the most normal thing in the world and put them back in the box."

"Did he say something crude?"

Another flush of heat warmed her cheeks. "No, not at all, but I could see it in his face."

"See what?"

She threw her hands in the air. "I don't know. Amusement, maybe. He was making fun of me in his mind. I know he was, and that bothers me. It shouldn't bother me, but..."

"Hold on." Emily patted her leg. "Let's analyze this before we jump to any conclusions. How did you react when you realized your vibrator was on the floor somewhere?"

"I panicked. I tried to get him to stop helping, but it was too late. He already had it in his hand."

Emily nodded. "Are you sure he was amused at the vibrator and condoms? Or do you think he could have found your reaction funny?"

"Well, I...I guess it could have been my reaction. I don't know. I was so embarrassed." She dragged her hands down her face.

"It's not like he thought you were a virgin. What's there to be embarrassed about?"

Trish toyed with the loose tape on the box. "You're right. I'm a grown woman; I shouldn't be embarrassed that he knows I have sex with other men...and with myself. It's just..." She glanced at the door and lowered her voice. "Is it weird that the fact he touched my vibrator turns me on? Like, next time I use it, I'm going to be thinking about that."

Emily laughed. "That's not weird at all. You're

attracted to him; he adores you. He's probably in his apartment right now fantasizing about you using it."

Now there was a mental picture worth imagining. "Do you think he ever thinks about me when he…"

"I'd put money on it."

Trish shot to her feet and shook her arms, trying to chase away the tingling sensation spreading through her body. "This isn't helping. I don't want to talk about Eric anymore."

"Okay. You said the box got knocked off the bed. Care to elaborate on that?"

She shrugged. "Eric said it was the ghost, but I probably just set it too close to the edge."

"Or maybe someone was trying to get your attention."

"There are better ways of doing it than by making a mess." Trish straightened her spine. "If a spirit knocked that box over, you need to stop. I'm the new lady of the house, and I will not tolerate this home or anything in it being damaged. Do you understand?"

Emily cringed. "Way to provoke before we even know what we're dealing with."

"They have to respect me." The moment she uttered the last word, a stack of boxes three-high toppled over.

Her heart dropped into her stomach before it ricocheted up into her throat. She squealed and clutched Emily's arm, dragging her toward the door as she flung it open. "Who did that? Did you see anything?"

"No, and I definitely won't if you pull me out of the room." She tugged from her grasp. "Give me a second."

Footsteps pounded on the stairs, and Trish spun around to find Eric racing toward them. "Are you okay? What happened?" He rested a hand on her shoulder, his concerned gaze traveling first over her face, then down her body and back to her eyes.

"I'm fine. I think we're going to let Emily do her thing before I unpack though." She took a deep breath. Eric's touch soothed her, and her heart finally returned to her chest where it belonged.

"Why did you scream?" He removed his hand from her shoulder, and his gaze locked on the fallen boxes. "Did you...?"

"Trish provoked the ghost." Emily walked around the room, holding out her arms as if searching the air for something. "Whoever is here didn't like her proclamation of being the lady of the house."

"Is it a former owner?" he asked.

"I don't know." Emily closed her eyes, her chest rising and falling as she took three deep breaths.

Trish stilled. She'd seen her friend in spirit hunting mode before. When she couldn't see a ghost in the room, she listened. After two more deep inhales, Emily's brow furrowed. She tilted her head, her face scrunching in concentration. "Can you say that again? You're not coming through clearly."

Holy crap. She found someone. Trish held her breath, and her heart rate kicked up again. She shouldn't have been surprised. Just about every building in New Orleans had a ghost story attached to it. Some of them were nothing more than legend, but plenty more were real. Ghosts couldn't hurt people, though. Not outright anyway. Strong ones could knock stuff over, move objects, but if they tried to harm a person, their form would pass right through. Both Emily and Sean promised her that.

She had nothing to be afraid of, but her nerves overre-acted anyway. She was light-headed, and her stomach soured as her muscles began to tremble. Was that a whisper in her right ear? *Oh, dear lord.* Now she was hearing things. The whooshing sound was most likely her blood pulsing in her veins.

There it was again. The raspy cadence sounded way too much like a voice for it to be Trish's own blood. It started in her right ear, and then it felt as if it passed through her skull to whisper in her left.

She sucked in a massive breath. Her anxiety would not get the better of her. Not now. Not in front of Eric.

He cleared his throat and looked at his arm, where Trish clutched his bicep, her nails digging into his skin. She jerked her hand away and mouthed *sorry.* Another deep breath and her pulse slowed to a normal rate. She focused on her surroundings, grounding herself in the moment like her therapist had taught her, and the tension slowly drained away.

Emily opened her eyes. "Whoever it is, they used up all their energy moving the boxes. They're not coming through."

Trish righted the bottom box and slid it against the wall. *Whew. That was close.* She hadn't had a panic attack in nearly a year, and she wasn't about to start now. "Did you hear anything?"

"I think I might have heard the word 'curse,' but I'm not positive."

Eric picked up the second box and froze. "Seriously?"

Trish took it from his hands and set it on the floor next to the others. "Why do you sound like that means something? Do you think this house is cursed?"

He raked a hand through his hair. "When Blake read the disappointments room, he sensed a woman muttering something about a curse."

Emily nodded. "That's probably what I heard then."

Trish's gaze bounced between Eric and Emily. "Curses aren't real, are they? I mean, ghosts, sure. Your life energy has to go somewhere when it leaves your body, but people don't have the power to magically harm others, do they?"

Her friends looked at each other, neither one of them answering the question. Her stomach soured. "They can't do that, can they, Em?"

"Someone summoned a demon and trapped it in a box. It killed my sister, and it almost killed Sean." Her shoulders crept toward her ears. "If they can do that..."

Trish sank onto the bed. "Ghosts I can handle, but a curse? How can I live in a house that's cursed?"

"Hold on." Eric lifted his hands, his palms toward her. "Let's not jump to any conclusions. Most 'curses' are self-fulfilling." He made air quotes. "When people get it in their heads that they're cursed, they blame every little thing that goes wrong on a magic spell that usually doesn't exist."

"That's true," Emily said. "The mind is powerful, and a strong belief in something passed down through the generations can be self-fulfilling, like Eric said. If a person struggles with mental illness like an anxiety disorder, their thoughts about a curse—even one that doesn't exist—could potentially drive them mad."

"Great." She flung her hands into the air before dropping them in her lap. "You know I have anxiety."

"Which is why you need to stay calm." Emily sat next to her. "Most of the outlandish tales of the paranormal can be explained if you think logically and you don't let your emotions get the better of you."

"Your demon was real."

"And we haven't encountered one since." She looked at Eric. "Have you come across one on your investigations?"

"Nope. That's the first and only true case of the demonic I've ever witnessed."

Trish clasped her hands. "How do y'all do it? How do you stay so calm and logical about stuff like this?"

"I'm sorry. Have we met?" Emily laughed. "Logic is kinda my thing."

"With my ability, if I didn't think logically, *I'd* go insane," Eric said.

"Yeah, you're right. If people think they're cursed, they act like they're cursed. I have nothing to do with the history of this house so I'm not going to worry about it." And why should she? Her anxiety was under control, thanks to her medication. Worrying about a curse that might or might not exist would make it one of those self-fulfilling things her friends mentioned. She stood and squared her shoulders. "Do you want to check out the rest of the house and see if you can make contact with anyone?"

"Of course." Emily rose and strode into the hallway.

Trish and Eric followed her from room to room, silently waiting as she searched. But in every space she entered, she shook her head and said she found nothing.

"This is where the disappointments room was," Trish said. "If there are any ghosts who want to talk, I bet they'll be in here."

"This is where the room *is*." Eric ran his hand over the new wall, his expression solemn. "It's still there."

"Why don't y'all wait downstairs?" Emily stepped toward the wall and rested her palm against it. "The spirits haven't seen the living in decades, so they might be intimidated by a group. Let me see if I can make contact alone."

"Is that safe?" Eric asked. "Sean will kill me if anything happens to you."

Emily laughed. "I'm so glad you have confidence in me, Eric."

"I didn't mean it like that."

"Eric has a protective nature." Trish gave him a wink. "He can't help how he was raised."

"I haven't sensed anything negative since I got here," Emily said. "If I do, I'll let you know."

Trish and Eric descended the stairs to wait in the living room. He sat on the sofa, and she took the chair adjacent to it, curling one leg beneath her and facing her body toward him. Eric's protectiveness was one of the reasons she felt safe in this house. At the slightest sound of distress, he would come running to rescue her. He'd proven that already.

"Do you really not believe in curses?" She rested her elbow on the arm of the chair.

"I don't know." He shrugged before looking into her eyes. "I believe anything is possible. You just have to want it enough."

The intensity in his eyes gave her goosebumps. Why did she feel like he wasn't talking about curses? "What about the opposite? I *don't* want it enough, so it isn't going to happen to me."

He laughed dryly. "I suppose it can work both ways."

"The house is definitely haunted," Emily said as she came down the stairs. "But no one is interested in making contact right now. I can try again in a few days, maybe bring Sean with me, but I don't sense anything danger-ous." She stopped on the bottom step and leaned her arm on the rail. "You probably just pissed off a former lady of the house when you proclaimed the home to be yours, but you're right in claiming the space. They need to know who's in charge."

A prickling sensation crawled up Trish's back, making her shiver as she moved toward her friend. A hot bath with lavender oil was in order tonight. She needed to chill the eff out. "Is there anything I should do in the meantime to protect myself?"

"Salt and sage are your friends. Smudge all the rooms, and if they bother you at night, put a ring of salt around your bed. Once they get used to you, they might be more willing to talk, and then maybe we can find out why they're still here."

"So I'm safe?"

"From human spirits, yes. Like I said, I didn't sense anything evil. Just pay attention and be careful." Her eyes tightened. "If there truly is a curse, I'm afraid Sean and I can't help you. It's worth looking into just in case."

She could deal with a few ornery ghosts. A curse was a different story.

"I'm going to do some more research about the people who lived here," Eric said. "I want to find out what happened to all these women. Evil entities can hide, and I want to be *sure* you're safe here."

Trish put her hands on her hips. "Okay, but don't think about it too much. I don't want you manifesting something that could interfere with my plans. Curse or no curse, I'm staying and running this business whether the spirits like it or not."

CHAPTER NINE

"No! Let me out!" Trish sat bolt upright in bed, her hands fisted in the tangled sheets. Her breaths came in short pants, and her heart beat so hard she could feel each pulse of blood as it pumped through her body.

She inhaled deeply, trying to slow her breathing as visions of the nightmare rolled through her mind. An invisible force held her down, pinning her to the floor and making icy panic course through her veins. Then the dream changed, and she stood upright in a tiny wooden room. She banged against the walls, scratching at them, the scents of dirt and decay making her feel as if she'd been buried alive.

As the churning nausea in her gut settled, she shook the image from her mind and crawled on her hands and knees to peer over the edge of the bed. The salt ring Emily had instructed her to use was intact, which meant no ghosts had caused the frightening dreams. That or her friend must have left out the psychic incantation she needed to bless the stuff with because it didn't do a lick of good. This nightmare was even worse than the last.

Her imagination had been running wild all week after Emily's visit and talk of a possible curse. Some deep breathing and an occasional dose of Ativan had helped to keep her anxiety in check during the day, but it had come out in full force the past three nights in a row, as if the seed of the nightmare had been planted while she was awake and it only bloomed when she slept.

As she untangled the sheets, the same raspy whisper she'd been imagining since the day she moved in sounded on her right side. She pressed her hands to her ears as if she could force it to cease, but the sound only intensified as she muffled the outside noises. That meant the whisper was coming from inside her, right? Her mind must've been fabricating the sensation.

"It's fine. I'm fine." She took one more deep breath and swung her legs over the side of the bed. A shadow crossed in front of the doorway, and she rubbed her eyes. Her imagination had also loaned her the sudden ability to see ghosts because shadows had been passing in the corners of her vision all week. It was absolutely ridiculous, of course. Trish didn't have a psychic bone in her body, but her mind was doing its best to scare the bejeezus out of her. "It's not going to work, brain. Give it up."

She stretched and glanced at the clock. *Holy crap.* The contractors were due to arrive in five minutes. After throwing on a bra beneath her tank top—she couldn't have the workers getting a view of her nips—she shot down the stairs to open the house.

Her shoulder jerked as a prickling sensation crawled up her back, and she rubbed her neck before unlocking the door. That had happened several times since she moved in too. Could it be a ghost trying to get her attention, or was that her overactive imagination as well?

She opened the door and found the crew waiting in their truck outside. "Come on in, guys. What are we working on today?"

Luke, the team leader, nodded a hello as he stepped onto the porch. "Your master bath is first on the list. Then we'll work on the rest of the plumbing upstairs. We'll have to shut off the water to the main house."

Well, crap. She couldn't go all day with no shower. At the very least, she needed to brush her teeth. "What about the garage apartment?"

"That's on a separate line, so it will still be running."

"Good."

Eric lay in bed, a thin sheet covering him and the ceiling fan whirring above. Soft morning sunlight filtered in through the blinds, making the windows almost appear to glow in the darkness of his apartment. He needed to get up and start the day, but his head felt heavy and his body refused to cooperate.

Five more minutes. He'd give himself a little time, then this foggy, groggy sensation would lift and he'd haul his ass out of bed.

It was no wonder he was exhausted. Thanks to the information he'd obtained about all the deaths in the mansion, his usual sweet dreams about Trish were replaced by nightmares involving curses and murder.

It had taken him nearly a week to gather all the information. Between meetings with the contractors, his marketing guy, and getting his business license so he could get his theater up and running, he'd been pressed for time. Trish said she hadn't noticed any more unusual activity in the house, but he checked in on her every day, opening his senses to feel if any negative emotions emanated from the spirits. So far, he'd found nothing. Whoever was haunting the place, they were good at hiding.

A soft knock sounded on his door, and he forced his eyes open. The clock on the wall read nine a.m. He groaned. It was probably the contractor here to tell him they found another issue and the renovation price would be even higher.

The person knocked again, and he sat up, wiping the sleep from his eyes. "I'm coming." He grabbed a pair of shorts from his dresser and threw them on before padding to the door. He yanked it open, but his irritation dissolved when he found Trish standing on the landing.

She wore pajama shorts and a yellow tank top, and her hair was disheveled from sleep. Her face was free of makeup, and as her gaze traveled down his body, his chest tightened at the sight of her. She looked exactly how he'd imagined her waking up next to him.

"Did I wake you?" She moistened her lips, her gaze dropping to his chest again.

"No, I was up," he lied.

"Can I use your shower? They're working on my bathroom today, and they shut off the water to the main house. They said it should still be working here."

He blinked, finally coming out of his haze. Trish had a set of clothes draped over her arm, and she carried a small overnight bag.

"Yeah. Of course." He stepped aside to let her enter and ground his teeth, biting back the *Mind if I join you?* he would have said had he not promised to stop flirting.

"Thanks." She stood in his living room and looked around, taking in the pale blue walls, crown molding, and new furniture. She cocked her head at the fireplace before looking at him. "This is nice. I don't know why I imagined a ratty couch with cinderblocks and plywood for a coffee table."

Ouch. "Because you can't get past your image of me to see the real man. I'm not some spoiled punk with no sense of responsibility."

Her mouth hung open. "I never said you were."

"You didn't have to. The bathroom is here." He brushed past her and grabbed his toothbrush from its holder on the sink. "I'll get dressed and be in the main house so I don't disturb you."

"You don't have to leave."

He strode into his bedroom and closed the door. After throwing on a t-shirt and some shoes, he returned to the hallway. Trish already had the shower running, so he brushed his teeth at the kitchen sink, filled a pitcher with water, and carried it to the mansion.

Her jabs about his age and maturity were beyond old. He didn't mind the jokes from the rest of the crew much because he knew they were only kidding. They showed him respect, treated him like an equal. Though Trish tried to act like she was joking, she really believed he was nothing more than a kid.

He set the pitcher on the counter and opened the pantry door to grab the coffee. Trish had told him he was welcome to anything in the kitchen, but he hadn't made himself that much at home yet. He had everything he needed in his apartment, so this was his first peek into Trish's food stash.

She had two kinds of Pop-Tarts, strawberry and

brown sugar cinnamon, a box of fruity cereal, and a pack of Twinkies. *Who's the kid now?* He chuckled, grabbing the can of coffee grounds and the brown sugar Pop-Tarts. After setting up the coffee machine, he dropped the pastries into the toaster. He waited for the coffee to be ready before pressing the toast lever. Then, he settled at the breakfast table with his shots of caffeine and sugar.

He finished the first Pop-Tart as Trish padded into the kitchen. Her skin was pink from the shower, and a stray lock of damp hair fell across her forehead. She set her bag on the counter, poured herself a cup, and sank into a chair next to him. "I'm sorry for saying that earlier. I don't think you're a spoiled punk, and I'm sorry I made you feel like I do."

Well, that defused his anger bomb quickly. Damn, she was good at apologies. "It's irritating, you know. I'm doing everything I can to prove myself to you, but you don't see me. You've created this idea of who I am in your head, and I can't compete with your imagination."

Whoa. He did not intend to spill his guts to her this morning. He shoved a piece of Pop-Tart into his mouth to stop from saying more.

"You don't have to prove anything to me, and I do see you. The jokes are..." She took a sip of coffee, staring at the table for a moment before looking into his eyes. "They're a defense mechanism, okay?"

"Defense against what?"

"You know what." She stood and paced to the pantry, grabbing a box of cereal and pouring it into a bowl before continuing. "We're attracted to each other. You answered the door half-naked, so I had to do something to stifle the sexual tension hanging between us." She returned to the table and shoveled a spoonful of Fruit Loops into her mouth.

He started to respond, but the words lodged in his throat. "That's..."

"Not the right way to do it. I know, and I'm sorry."

Without his empathic ability, he wasn't sure how she felt about his state of undress when he opened the door this morning. Her facial expressions and body language had said she liked what she saw, but he'd doubted himself. He needed to stop doing that. "What are we going to do about the situation? Because I don't think the sexual tension is going away anytime soon." Not on his end, anyway.

"I'm going to find ways to defuse it without insulting you. Otherwise, we're not going to do anything. This is a workplace environment, and I will not risk my new career by trying to be anything other than friends."

"Technically, we don't work together. We're just sharing the same building."

"A building that belongs to your grandmother, the person who could end my contract with only a month's notice. She's protective of you, and if something bad happened between us, I don't doubt she would kick me out."

"She wouldn't..." He wouldn't let her.

"Eric." She sighed. "Listen, you're not the only one who feels like you have to prove yourself. Have you not wondered where I got the money to afford a place like this? I wasn't exactly making bank at the urgent care clinic."

He shrugged. "I was curious, but I figured it was none of my business, so I didn't ask."

"Well, I'm going to tell you so you will understand

why we can't date." She took another bite of cereal and then a sip of coffee, making his anticipation build.

"My dad was wealthy, and my stepmother wanted him all to herself. She never liked me, and when he died, she took every opportunity she could get to let me know I would never amount to anything because my dad spoiled me."

"That's awful."

She nodded. "He passed away when I was eighteen. Luckily, I was a legal adult so the money he left me went into a trust, and my stepmother couldn't spend it. She did hold the purse strings, though. Anytime I wanted to make a withdrawal, she had to approve it until I turned thirty."

"I hear that's fairly common with trusts." His was set up the same way.

"Yeah, well, when I moved to New Orleans, she told me I was crazy, that I would fail and be back within a year, and that if I didn't come back, I wouldn't see a penny of my dad's money until I had full control of the trust."

"She sounds like a lovely woman."

Trish laughed dryly. "Tell me about it. But I was young and in love, and even though my boyfriend didn't ask me to move to New Orleans with him, I followed him. He dumped me a week later."

"That bastard."

She smiled, holding his gaze, and the sexual tension she was trying to avoid sizzled between them. The urge to lean in and kiss her had him holding his mug in a death grip.

"What?" He asked rather than giving in to the urge.

"Nothing." She ate another bite of her cereal. "Anyway, I couldn't very well run back to Texas and let my stepmother know she was right. So I hunkered down in

New Orleans, went to school, got a job, and busted my ass to prove that I could make it on my own."

"You know, you don't need to prove yourself to her. You are an adult and can live your life the way you choose."

"I know. But when you're told you'll never amount to anything enough times, you start to believe it. I'm not trying to prove anything to her anymore. I'm proving it to myself." She sipped her coffee. "I tend to make snap decisions, and things rarely work out the way I plan. Your grandma giving me a second chance at running this house is a dream come true, and I'm not going to risk ruining it."

"I think you're doing great."

"Thank you, but can you see why making this bed and breakfast successful is so important to me? I like you, Eric. I always have, but I refuse to get burned again. There's too much at stake."

He wanted to argue that he would never hurt her, but, based on his track record with women, he couldn't make that guarantee, could he? She was aware of his reputation. It was no wonder she wanted to steer clear of him.

He drummed his fingers on the table. *You know what? That's bullshit.* It was true he didn't stay in relationships for long, but that was because of his ability. Trish was different. It would be different with her, and he would prove it to her. He'd start by being the best friend she'd ever had. "We'll keep it in the friend zone as long as you stop treating me like a kid."

"Deal. And for the record, I really don't think you're a kid. You're the reason I feel safe here, even with the ghosts and the possible curse."

Good. That was exactly how he wanted her to feel. Even as nothing more than friends, her safety in this house was his number one priority. "Speaking of the possible curse, I found something in my research."

"Please don't tell me it's real. Not after I opened my heart to you and told you how much all this means to me." She smiled, but it didn't reach her eyes.

"I don't have any proof that it's real, but the woman who murdered her daughter and then killed herself back in the eighties left behind a note. It said, 'I have to end the curse.'"

"You've got to be kidding me." Trish shifted in her seat, her appetite for her favorite sugary cereal suddenly turning sour. "The news reports said she was a paranoid schizophrenic."

The seller had disclosed the violent crime that happened in the house, but it was nearly forty years ago. Trish assumed whatever spirit energy that remained from the incident would have dissipated in four decades, and if it didn't, she had plenty of contacts of the psychic variety who could help clear it. Honestly, the entire city had a sordid history. She expected whatever house she purchased would've had some kind of tragic event in its past. She hadn't been the slightest bit worried...until now.

"That was in the official report, yes. I don't think they released the contents of the note to the press. Otherwise, this house would have wound up on a haunted history tour."

"How did you find out if it wasn't released?"

"My family has connections."

"Of course you do." She crossed her arms and tapped her foot. "Curses are just self-fulfilling prophecies. Both you and Emily said that." Although, a curse would explain the nightmares she'd endured this week. They did make her feel a bit like she was going crazy. No. No, it wouldn't. Her bad dreams were created by her own mind, end of story.

"Most of them are, but Voodoo is strong in New Orleans. Most practitioners are kind, peaceful people, but there are bad ones, just like in any population. I highly doubt there's a curse on the house, but anything is possible."

Her skin crawled, and she rubbed the back of her neck. "So, let's call Natasha and ask her to break the curse. If there's one here, I'm sure she can take care of it. The woman can banish demons."

"That's not a bad idea. At the very least, it'll ease your worry, so it doesn't become self-fulfilling for you."

"I'm not going to think myself into madness." She was way too smart for that.

A thud sounded from across the kitchen, and she turned to find three cabinet doors wide open. "Did you do that?"

"Do what?"

She glanced at him, and when she returned her gaze to the kitchen, all the doors were closed. "The cabinet doors. They were open and then closed. You didn't hear it?" He had to have. The sound was unmistakable.

Eric turned in his seat to look into the kitchen. "I didn't hear anything. Are you…?"

"Am I what?" She drummed her fingers on the table, chewing her bottom lip. He was kidding. He had to be.

"I was going to ask if you're sure, but if you saw it, you saw it. I believe you."

"Well, I…" She did see the doors open, didn't she?

Not the actual movement, no. They were open, and then they were closed. She heard a thud, though, right? But that could have been the contractors. Damn it, now she wasn't sure what she saw, but if those ghosts were messing with her…

She shot to her feet. "You had your chance to speak to me when Emily was here. Now you'll just have to wait until next time. Leave this house alone."

She plopped into her chair and found Eric grinning at her. "What?"

He chuckled. "I'm admiring your bravery. Most people without abilities are terrified of spirits."

"They're just people without bodies." She shrugged.

"You should come on a ghost hunt with us."

"Y'all do just fine without me. Do you have Natasha's number?" She wanted to get this taken care of as soon as possible. Whether it was ghosts, a curse, or her imagination, she would conquer it. She just needed to know which she was dealing with so she could formulate a plan of action.

"I'll have to ask Sean. Let me send him a text." He tugged his phone from his pocket and typed on the screen.

Trish sipped her coffee and admired the strong line of his jaw as he stared at his phone. He'd filled out a lot since she'd first met him three years ago, his boyish good looks transforming into mature, handsome features. She would try harder not to poke fun at his age. It was a sore spot for him, and she should have recognized that a long time ago. Besides, everything he'd said and done since they started on this adventure together had indicated a level of maturity beyond his years. He was a hell of a lot more mature than her last date, anyway.

"Got it. I'll put it on speaker." He laid the phone on the table and pressed the call button.

It rang four times before Natasha picked up. "Hello?"

"Hey, Natasha." He leaned toward the phone. "This is Eric and Trish from Crescent City Ghost Tours. How are you today?"

"Hello," Trish said.

"I'm wonderful," Natasha said. "I'd ask how you two are, but I sense you've got a problem."

"Damn, she's good," Trish muttered.

Natasha laughed. "What other reason would you be calling for?"

"Good point." She straightened and looked at Eric.

He held her gaze for a moment, grinning before he spoke, "We were hoping you could come out to a new property we purchased and see if it might be cursed."

"*We* didn't purchase it," Trish said. "Eric's grandma did, and we're renting out the space for completely separate businesses. It's not... I mean, we're not..." She clamped her mouth shut. *Get a grip, woman. He meant "we," as in him and his grandma, not us.*

Eric's grin widened, and shuffling sounded on the other end of the line before Natasha replied, "What makes you think the house is cursed?"

"Both Blake and Emily picked up the word when they were doing readings here," Eric said, "and the last death in the house involved a suicide note about ending a curse."

"We need you to get rid of it." Trish rested her forearms on the table and leaned toward the phone. "It makes the women in the house go crazy."

"Mm-hmm. That sounds like a doozy. I can come out tomorrow morning and take a look. How's nine a.m. sound?"

"That sounds great." Eric winked at Trish, and her stomach fluttered. "Thank you so much, Natasha."

"Text me the address. See y'all tomorrow."

"Are you going to be okay staying here another night?" Unease clouded his eyes, and his concern for her safety turned the flutter in her belly into a swarm of butterflies.

Deflect, Trish. It is not happening with him. "Let me guess. You're going to suggest I need a big, strong man here to protect me?"

He blinked, his brow lifting. "Considering you asked me not to say things like that anymore, no. I wasn't suggesting that at all."

Damn. He was doing a much better job at this "being friends" gig than she was. She tucked her hair behind her ear. "I'll be fine. No little curse is going to drive me away from achieving my goals." Though she might pick up a dream catcher while she was out, just to be safe.

Eric stood and put his coffee mug in the sink. "If you run into any trouble tonight, I'm just a few yards away. Call me."

That she knew, and the idea was far too tempting.

CHAPTER TEN

Scrambled eggs bubbled in a frying pan as Eric finished chopping the tomato. He flipped the eggs and sprinkled the cheese and other fillings on one side before folding it over and sliding it onto a plate. He had no idea how Natasha's reading would go this morning, but one thing was certain. Trish needed more than sugar and caffeine in her system if the news was bad.

He could hear her moving around in her bedroom upstairs, and with the Voodoo priestess due to arrive in half an hour, she should be down any minute. The coffee maker beeped, and he took two mugs from the newly installed cabinet before running his hand over the oak door. The kitchen was one part of the house guests wouldn't see, so they'd installed top-of-the-line appliances, granite countertops, and solid wood cabinetry. It was the most modern-looking room in the entire house, yet the color palette and simple design of the woodwork didn't clash with the nineteenth-century vibe the rest of the home would have.

"What are you doing?" Trish stopped in the entryway, her brow furrowing in confusion.

He carried her plate to the table and pulled out a chair. "It's about time you had a grown-up breakfast, don't you think?"

She shuffled toward the table and sank into the seat he offered, her gaze taking in the spread of toast, strawberry and peach preserves, assorted berries, and orange juice. "You made all this?"

"We need our strength up when Natasha gets here. She might want us to participate in some kind of ritual." He poured the coffee and set two mugs on the table before grabbing his omelet from the counter.

"A ritual?" She draped a napkin across her lap.

"You never know." He shrugged and took a bite of omelet.

Her smile reached all the way to her eyes. "Thank you. This was very sweet of you." She buttered a piece of toast and spread strawberry preserves across it before taking a bite. "This is delicious."

"It's what my grandma serves at Landry House. She sources everything from local small businesses."

"I love that. I'll have to get the names of the people she uses. I'd like to do that here too." She took a bite of omelet and closed her eyes. "Mmm... These eggs taste fresh."

"Local free-range chicken farm." He couldn't fight his smile. Seeing her enjoying the meal he prepared for her warmed him from the inside out.

She moaned as she swallowed and then sipped her coffee. "Careful. A girl could get used to this. Don't spoil me."

"I can't help how I was raised." He looked into her eyes and held her gaze.

"You're full of surprises, aren't you?" A magnetism charged between them so thick he could have cut it with her jam-covered knife.

"Not really." He cleared his throat and broke eye contact before that damn urge to lean in and kiss her made him do something he shouldn't. After her story about her stepmom and the asshole she moved here for, he understood why she didn't want to get involved with him. It sucked royally, but he understood.

"Eat up." He picked up his orange juice. "Natasha will be here soon."

She ate a few more bites and set her fork on the plate. "How did you sleep?"

"Like a rock. You?"

She shook her head. "I keep having nightmares. I'm sure it's my overactive imagination. Thinking about what happened in the disappointments room makes me feel a little sick. I have a diagnosed anxiety disorder. If I'd been alive in the 1800s, there's a good chance I'd have been locked in a room like that."

"You're too strong to end up with a man who would treat you like that."

Her lips twitched before she bit her bottom one. "Women didn't have many choices back then."

"You do now. Hopefully the dreams will go away once you get used to the house."

She drummed her fingers on the table. "I've also been seeing things."

"What things?"

"Shadows and movement out of the corner of my eye.

I mean, obviously, there are ghosts here, but I can't tell if that's what I'm seeing or if it's my imagination again."

"If it makes you feel better, most places we investigate have claims like that. Ninety percent of the time, it's people's overactive imaginations. It's the most common claim we hear, even though most people can't see spirits."

"I hear whispers." She swallowed hard.

"Old houses make all kinds of weird noises. It's probably in the pipes. And don't forget the contractors are in and out all day. We can usually debunk claims of weird noises too."

She laughed, but there wasn't much humor in it. "So I'm not going crazy?"

"Not at all."

"I also keep getting this weird skin-crawling sensation. I don't know." She waved a hand before laying it on the table. "It's probably psychosomatic."

"I'm sure once Natasha gets here and lays this curse business to rest, you'll feel like a brand-new woman." He rested his hand on hers. "Don't worry, okay?"

"You always know the right thing to say, don't you?"

"I say what I mean."

They ate in comfortable silence, and when Trish finished the last bite on her plate, he carried them both to the sink. She gathered the other dishes from the table and helped him clean the mess, sharing the space with him as if they'd done this a hundred times.

He stole a glance at her as she put the jars of preserves into the fridge, and when she turned around and caught him looking, she smiled. "Thank you again for all of this. It was the most delicious breakfast I think I've ever had."

"Wait 'til you taste my shrimp and grits. It's an old family recipe."

She cocked her head, looking at him like she was *seeing* him again. His chest tightened, and he swallowed the thickness from his throat before turning around and loading the dishwasher. The doorbell chimed at nine a.m. on the dot, filling the house with its deep, melodious tune.

He dried his hands on a dishtowel. "You ready for this?"

"To lift a curse? Absolutely."

Eric opened the door and motioned for the priestess to enter. "Good morning, Natasha. Thanks for coming out on such short notice."

"Anything for the Ghost Tours crew. Y'all send plenty of business to my Voodoo shop, don't you?" She paused before entering, running her gaze around the door frame. Her dark brown hair was woven into braids and twisted into a large bun on top of her head. She wore a royal blue tunic, and her matching skirt swished around her ankles as she crossed the threshold.

"Yes, ma'am, we do." He closed the door and followed her through the foyer and into the front parlor.

"It's good to see you again, Trish." Natasha ran her hand along the wall before resting both palms on the back of a burgundy-upholstered chair. "Has Emily heard any more from her sister?"

Trish shook her head. "I think Jessica returned to where she's supposed to be."

When Eric first joined Crescent City Ghost Tours, Emily's late sister had contacted her through Sean to warn her about a dybbuk box she'd acquired. That was the first and only time Eric had heard about a real demonic entity. Most of the evil in the world was committed by the living.

"Good to hear." Natasha set a large burlap bag on the

chair. "I'd like to walk through the house and see what I pick up. Y'all are welcome to follow me."

"Lead the way," Trish said.

They followed Natasha throughout the first floor, her expression becoming more solemn and disturbed as she read the energy in the house. When they reached the upstairs, she gasped and stopped on the landing, shaking her head.

Trish gave Eric a worried look. "Is it bad? Can you clear it?"

The priestess ignored her questions and disappeared into a bedroom.

"She doesn't look happy," Trish whispered.

"No, she doesn't." Eric stepped into the room and dropped his shields to soak in Natasha's emotions. He caught a quick burst of nauseating disgust before her energy slammed into him, knocking him back a step.

"I'll tell you what I think when I'm done with my walk-through," she chided. "You try a stunt like that on me again, and I'll leave you both without an answer. Are we clear, young man?"

Eric lowered his head. "Yes, ma'am. I apologize."

Natasha brushed past him to go to the next room, and Trish elbowed him. "What were you doing?" she whispered through her teeth.

He shrugged and lifted his hands. He was an empath. Reading people was his nature, but he should have known better than to try it on the person with the strongest psychic abilities he'd ever encountered.

"Come in here," Natasha called, and he and Trish paced into the room.

She laid her hands against the new wall and shook her

head. "You've got another room in here. A bad room. Bad energy."

"We know," he said. "That's a new wall."

She looked at Trish and then at him before sighing in disappointment and moving on to the next space. After doing her thing in all the second-floor rooms, she returned to the parlor and sank into a chair. Eric and Trish followed suit.

"There's a lot of residual energy built up in this house. Lotta pain, lotta suffering."

That didn't surprise him in the least. "Can you clear it?"

She nodded. "I'll do a blessing. It'll get rid of what the living here left behind, and you should feel better." She looked at Trish. "You're lucky you're not a sensitive. You'd a been feeling it if you were."

Trish swallowed hard and glanced at Eric.

"You have been feeling it." Natasha shook her head. "There are ghosts here, but they're not coming forward. I sense mental unrest in them, and I don't believe they have the capacity to communicate."

"Can you get rid of them?" she asked.

"I have a friend who could force them out, but they need their story told first if they're to rest in peace."

Eric's jaw tightened. He knew they shouldn't have sealed off the disappointments room. His gut had told him exactly what Natasha said.

"What about the curse?" Trish asked. "Is it real?"

"I'm afraid it is, and it's what's keeping the ghosts here. They were all affected by it in life." She pulled a bundle of sage out of her bag and stood. "You two, go open all the windows and doors. I'm going to smudge the house and bless it. Then we'll see what's left."

They did as the priestess asked, opening the windows and letting in the summer heat. It didn't take long before the inside felt damp, but old houses like this were designed for optimum airflow. New Orleans was hot and humid long before they had central AC.

Natasha lit the sage and wafted the smoke through the rooms and around the windows and doors. She said the blessing in French, so he had no idea how she got rid of the energy, but as she snuffed out the bundle of herbs, the air felt lighter.

She instructed them to close all the windows, and then she shut the front door, completing the sanctification. "The blessing is done. I sensed most of the spirit energy was residual. I've cleared it, but there's an intelligent haunt here too. Otherwise, the house is a clean slate for you to build the energy however you like. When you're ready to cross the ghost over, call me."

"That's it?" Trish's voice sounded hopeful. "The curse is gone too?"

"No, child. That kind of blessing doesn't remove a curse."

"Will you?" Trish asked. "I'll pay you. Name the price."

Natasha shook her head. "This ain't about money. I can't remove a curse when I don't know what the curse is. I can feel it's there, but that's it. Whoever put it on this house was a powerful medium. It affects the living and the dead."

"So there's nothing we can do?" Trish asked.

"If you can find out who cursed the place and why, what was involved in the spell, then I can figure out how to break it. You should know, though, that most of the time, a hex this strong is only ended by the death of the person cursed."

Trish gasped. "The suicide note. That's what she meant."

"Given the history of the house," Natasha continued, "and the fact the curse is still present, I don't know what will end it."

"Is there any way we can find out?" Eric asked.

"Talk to the previous owners. See what they know about it and work your way backward."

Trish dropped onto the sofa. "The previous owner is dead."

Natasha gave them a sympathetic look. "Then it sounds like you've got a problem."

CHAPTER ELEVEN

"What are we going to do, Eric?" Trish stood in the foyer splaying her fingers and then fisting them, only to splay them again. "You heard Natasha. The curse is real. The women in this house go crazy."

"Hold on now. Let's not jump to conclusions." Eric gingerly took her arm and guided her into the kitchen to sit at the breakfast table. "We don't know the details of the curse. Maybe it affects the men of the house, and they drive the women crazy. Anybody would go insane being locked in that room."

Trish shook her head, her mind whirring with so many thoughts she couldn't keep up with them all as they bounced around inside her skull. "What are you saying? That it's going to make you mad, and you'll lock me up?" The octave of her voice raised with her panic.

He held up his hands in defense. "I'm not the man of this house. I live in the apartment over the garage, and I would *never* do anything like that to you. I think you know that."

"You would if a curse made you. After these night-mares and the things I've been seeing out of the corner of my eye, I'm starting to feel like I'm going insane. Natasha confirmed I don't have a psychically sensitive bone in my body. I'm not seeing ghosts, so what *am* I seeing?"

"Look." He pulled out his phone and typed on the screen. "I've got the closing documents in an email, and I'm sure it has the seller's phone number on it. Let's give her a call and see what she can tell us. It'll be a jumping point, and then we'll figure out what to do from there."

"Okay." Her palms grew slick, and she felt cold, clammy, and hot all at the same time. She couldn't tell if she was about to shiver or sweat, but her omelet was threatening to make a reappearance if she didn't calm herself down.

"Here it is. Rose Thompson." He rested his hand on top of hers. "We're going to figure this out. I'm not going to let anything happen to you."

The warmth of his touch took the edge off her nerves, and she had to wonder if his empathic ability didn't work both ways. "Are you sending me calming energy? Can you make people feel a certain way?"

He chuckled. "Now, that would be a great party trick. I wish I had that ability."

"Thank you for calming me down." She'd felt on the verge of hysteria for a hot minute, and she had no inten-tion of succumbing to this curse. Her pulse slowed with a deep breath. "How do you stay so collected? I've never even seen you scared."

"I hide it well." He squeezed her hand and let it go. "Ready to call Rose?"

"Yeah. The sooner the better." She crossed her legs and

clasped her hands, her muscles tensing as he dialed the number.

It rang five times before someone answered. "Hello?"

"May I speak to Rose Thompson?" Eric flicked his gaze to Trish and offered a small smile.

"Speaking. Who is this?"

"My name is Eric Landry. My grandmother purchased the Thompson mansion from you, and I was hoping to ask you a few questions. Do you have a moment?"

She paused, and the thump of a door closing sounded through the phone. "I can't tell you much. That was my uncle's place, and I want nothing to do with it. I put it up for sale the moment the estate passed to me."

Trish ground her teeth. If she wasn't concerned about a curse making her crazy, she'd have told this woman off for selling the place out from under her. Then again, Rose had inadvertently done her a favor. If Trish had bought the house, she'd be dealing with all this on her own.

"Would you mind talking about your aunt?" Eric asked, his voice gentle.

She let out a slow, heavy sigh. "What about her? She was a paranoid schizophrenic who murdered her only daughter—my cousin—and then killed herself. I'm very busy; I need to go."

Eric picked up the phone, holding it closer to his mouth. "Did she ever mention a curse?"

Rose scoffed. "Yeah. She claimed the house was cursed, but it wasn't. She was mentally ill and needed to be in a hospital, but my uncle refused to have her locked up. Something about breaking an ancestral tradition. That family was messed up."

"One more question, and I'll let you go," Eric said.

"Did your aunt ever mention where the supposed curse came from? Did she say *anything* about it?"

"I don't..." She sighed again. "That was so long ago."

Eric remained silent, and Trish held her breath. *Think, Rose. You've got to give us something.*

"I want to say she called it Delphine's curse. Yeah, that's what it was."

Trish's heart sank, and Eric's expression became unreadable. "Thank you for your time, Rose."

He hung up and set the phone on the table, his brow pinching as he screwed his mouth over to one side.

"That wasn't helpful at all." Trish leaned back in her chair. "I've been on the haunted history tour. Delphine LaLaurie's house is supposedly cursed. Rose's aunt blamed her mental illness on a ghost story. Fantastic."

And now they were back to square one. The LaLaurie house wasn't even in the Garden District. "I don't know what I was thinking. I had these grand delusions that I could run my own business, but this is obviously a sign from the universe. Maybe my stepmother was right. I can't believe—"

"Trish." His face held a wary expression. "I don't think she means Delphine LaLaurie."

"What other Delphine went crazy and murdered people?"

He pressed his lips together, shaking his head. "Do you remember when I told you my great-great-grandfather lost this house to a Thompson in a poker game?"

"Yes."

"And it was supposed to be a wedding gift for his daughter?"

"I remember. What's your point?"

"My great-great-grandmother's name was Delphine."

"Wait…" She leaned forward. "Are you saying…"

"We need to talk to my grandma. I have a feeling she knows about the curse."

———————

"This is crazy." Trish wiped her clammy palms on her jeans as Eric pulled his car into the driveway. "Surely your grandma wouldn't have asked me to run the house if she knew it was cursed."

He killed the engine and turned to her. "She would never do anything to hurt you intentionally, but she might have heard rumors. It's possible the story was passed down through the generations, and they stopped believing it was true."

"Then why wasn't it passed to you?"

"I don't know. Maybe *because* they stopped believing it. Maybe because I'm a man." He slid out of the car and closed the door.

Trish pulled down the visor to check her makeup. As suspected, her mascara had smudged beneath her right eye, so she took a tissue from her purse, wet it with her tongue, and cleaned up her face.

As she flipped the visor into place, Eric opened her door. He stood there with his arm extended, so she placed her hand in his and allowed him to help her from the car. She didn't *need* help getting out, but Eric seemed to enjoy doing gentlemanly things like this. Who was she to deny the man such a simple pleasure?

Okay, she enjoyed it too. She could admit as much.

When they reached the front porch, Eric opened the door and rested his hand on the small of her back to guide her inside. Betty Landry met them in the foyer and smiled, her gaze bouncing between them. She wore navy pants with a beaded cream blouse, and she'd swept her light blonde hair up in a perfect twist. "Good afternoon, you two."

"Hi, Mrs. Landry."

Eric dropped his hand from Trish's back. "Are any guests in the parlor? We've got some questions for you."

"They're all out for the day. Come on back." She led them through a house filled with antiques and period furniture, and Trish tried to imagine Eric as a little boy growing up in this place. Cast iron lamps sat atop dark wood tables, paintings of what must've been his ancestors adorned the walls, and porcelain sculptures occupied the shelves and mantles. Everything looked expensive and breakable. It was no wonder Eric was such a gentleman. He probably had to be on his best behavior at all times here.

"Have a seat, dear." Mrs. Landry gestured to a loveseat, so Trish sank onto the cushion, her back ramrod straight, her knees together, and her hands folded in her lap. She felt like *she* needed to be on her best behavior in a house like this, and she made a mental note to make her B and B feel warmer and more inviting.

"Eric, honey." His grandma sat in a chair across from Trish. "I put a fresh pitcher of tea in the fridge. Go pour us some."

"Yes, ma'am." He glanced at Trish before disappearing down the hall.

"How are the renovations going? Will you open on schedule?" She crossed her legs and rested her hands on her knee.

Trish cleared her throat. "It's all moving along." She'd let Eric lead the conversation they came here to have.

Asking the woman who'd made her dreams come true if she exposed Trish to a curse wouldn't be in her best interest.

"That's good to hear. And how are things between you and Eric? Is he behaving himself?"

She laughed. "He behaves better than any man I've ever met. You raised him right."

"Indeed, I did. He'll make a fine husband." She arched a brow, giving Trish a knowing look in typical alpha grandma fashion. Poor Eric. Betty had probably tried to set him up with all her friends' granddaughters over the years.

"I'm sure he will be a great husband for someone someday. He and I are just friends."

"Mm-hmm."

Eric returned to the parlor, balancing three glasses filled with iced tea in his hands. "What did I miss?"

Mrs. Landry opened a drawer and set three coasters on the coffee table. "I was just telling Trish that a Landry always gets what he wants. Isn't that true?"

Eric chuckled as he set the glasses down. "I suppose so." He moved to sit in a chair adjacent to the loveseat.

"Sit next to Trish so I can look at you both. I don't want to crane my neck." She picked up a glass and took a sip, watching him over the rim.

Eric paused mid-sit and glanced at Trish before letting out a slow breath and moving to the loveseat. He mouthed *sorry* to her, and she suppressed a smile.

"There. That's better." She set her glass on the coaster. "Now, what was so important that I had to tape my afternoon shows to watch later?"

Eric looked at Trish, and she nodded to encourage him. After the way he described her reaction to the secret room sealed inside the mansion, he'd have to approach the subject carefully. "We need to talk about the house."

"What about it?" Her smile was strained as if she knew what he was about to say.

"What else do you know about the disappointments room?"

Her expression blanked, a mask of stoicism falling over her features. "I told you we will never speak of it again."

"Grandma." Eric scooted to the edge of the seat. "I know Mr. Thompson had the room built because his wife went insane."

"Poor woman. They called it hysterics." She stood and paced toward an oil on canvas portrait hanging above the fireplace. "It's such a shame."

Trish squinted to read the small plaque at the bottom of the painting. The glare made it hard to see, but it looked like the first word was Delphine.

"Every lady of the house since was locked in that room until the last." He rose and paced toward her. "Do you know why that is?"

"I don't have the slightest—"

"Grandma." His voice was stern yet respectful at the same time, and it commanded her attention. Mrs. Landry stiffened, clasping her hands together and staring at the portrait.

"Tell us about the curse." He gently laid a hand on her shoulder, and her posture relaxed. "I'm afraid Trish's life might be in danger."

Her head snapped toward him. "Nonsense. She's not a Thompson."

"So you do know about the curse." Trish's nails dug into her palms as she squeezed her fists. That was the first time Eric had suggested her safety was in jeopardy. He might have only said it to get his grandma talking, but she couldn't help the sour sensation creeping from her stomach to her throat.

Mrs. Landry slowly turned toward Trish, her expression solemn. "It happened a long time ago. I would never put you in harm's way."

"Come talk to us." Eric gently took her arm and guided her back to her chair before sitting next to Trish.

"What is Delphine's curse?" Trish asked.

She paused, and Trish wondered if it was for dramatic effect like Eric tended to do or if she simply couldn't find the words. Finally, she spoke, "Oscar, Delphine's husband, was a drunk and a gambler. It's a wonder he didn't squander the entire family fortune." Her tone was even, her calm demeanor forced. "William Thompson wanted to ruin us. He was a wicked man."

"The curse, Grandma."

"Our family built that house. Francis Landry had this one constructed for Oscar and that one for his brother Paul." She picked up a throw pillow and held it against her chest. "It never should have passed to that family."

Trish's shoulders tensed. If Mrs. Landry was going to be this defensive, they might never get it out of her. She wanted to snap at the woman, tell her to get to the point, but Eric remained relaxed, so she followed his lead.

"When Paul moved out of state, Oscar bought the house. It was supposed to be a wedding gift for his daughter, who was recently engaged, and Delphine was devastated...no, livid...when he lost it in a poker game to our family rival. William gave the house to his son to rub salt into the wound." She spoke of her ancestors as if she were alive to witness the event.

"So Delphine cursed the house," Eric said gently, urging her to continue.

Mrs. Landry sighed. "Delphine didn't curse it."

"Who did?" Trish asked.

"Her servant. You have to understand how prevalent Voodoo was back then and how important family status was. Delphine had no recourse; the house belonged to Oscar, so she couldn't stop him from transferring the deed. Instead, she made sure the Thompsons would never be happy there."

"What was the curse supposed to do?" Eric asked.

"It cast madness on the lady of the house and on any Thompson woman who lived there." She squared her gaze on Eric. "The Thompsons built the disappointments room because of the curse. That's why that room is a stain on our family name. Because Delphine's servant cursed the Thompson women."

Mrs. Landry set the pillow aside and smoothed her pants. "But now that the house has returned to its rightful owners, all is well. The curse was on the Thompson women. No Thompsons, no curse."

"How do you know all these details?" Trish asked. "It's like you were there when it happened."

"Delphine kept journals."

Eric straightened. "Where are they?"

"The cedar chest in the old servants' quarters upstairs."

"Thank you." Eric stood. "Come on, Trish. Let's go find those journals."

She followed him up the grand staircase to the second-floor landing before they hung a right and made their way to the back of the house. He opened a narrow door to reveal another staircase, and he flipped a light switch as he made his way up.

"I thought servants usually lived in outbuildings back then." She stopped in the doorway of a small room, where a single lightbulb provided the only illumination in the heavy space. Boxes sat stacked against the far wall, and an old mirror with an ornate brass frame leaned against the adjacent one.

"This is where the lady's maid stayed. Because she worked so closely with the lady of the house, she lived inside." Eric shoved a box aside to reveal the cedar chest, but Trish stepped toward the mirror.

The silver beneath the glass was tarnished at the edges, giving it a spooky look, and her mind drifted to all the books she'd read and movies she'd seen with mirrors acting as portals for the dead. "Here's a haunting waiting to happen."

"Damn. They're written in French." Eric sat on the wood floor and flipped through the pages of a leather-bound journal.

"That's no good. I took Spanish in high school." She kneeled next to him and picked up another book. The cover felt smooth beneath her fingers, and the thick paper inside smelled musty.

"My grandma can read them." He turned a page and pointed to the top right corner. "She dated the entries. Let's look for the one from 1882. That's when the house changed hands."

Trish flipped through book after book, scanning the elegant script, her curiosity piquing. What would a woman of such high stature have written about back then? "You should have these translated and typed for future generations. Even if your descendants learn French, they probably won't be able to read the cursive."

"That's not a bad idea. It sure would be handy right

now, wouldn't it?" He closed the journal and set it on the stack of books they'd checked. "I'm sorry about my grandma. I assume she was pestering you about why we're not a couple."

Trish shrugged. "It's okay. Southern grandmothers are like that. I didn't take offense."

"At least you know she likes you."

Aside from their meeting when Trish decided to accept the offer, they hadn't spoken more than a few words to each other. "She hardly knows me."

He closed the journal in his hands. "She knows I like you."

"Obviously." She let out a nervous laugh and picked up another book. "You said 1882, right?"

"Yeah."

"Here it is." She handed him the journal.

"Awesome. Let's go see what it says." He returned the other volumes to the chest and closed it before they descended the steps and found Mrs. Landry in the kitchen. "Hey, Grandma. Will you look through this one and see if she wrote the details of the spell?"

"If you'd paid better attention in French class, you could read it yourself." She dried her hands on a dishtowel and sat at the breakfast table.

Trish smirked at Eric. "You took French, and you didn't even try to find the spell?"

"Could you read it if it were written in Spanish?"

"Good point." She sank into the chair across from Mrs. Landry and tried not to stare at her as she turned the pages.

Eric's grandma smiled wistfully, occasionally chuckling as she read the entries. What a treasure those journals must be. "Here it is." She pointed to a page. "It says

'Phillis created a curse to drive every Thompson woman in the house to madness.' Then she details the ritual and the ingredients in the spell. I suppose she wanted to be able to replicate it if her husband lost another piece of property."

"Oh, thank goodness." Trish's breath came out in a rush of relief. She'd always had an overactive imagination, and she felt light-headed with the knowledge she wasn't a target for the curse. "I thought I would have to give up my dreams for a hot minute."

"I told you I wouldn't put you in harm's way, dear." Mrs. Landry reached across the table to pat Trish's hand. "Eric, get me a piece of paper, and I'll write it down for you."

"Do you mind if I take the book?" he asked. "I want Natasha to look at it, and I'd hate for anything to get lost in translation."

She eyed him for a moment before relenting. "If anything happens to this book…"

"I'll make sure he takes good care of it," Trish said.

Mrs. Landry nodded. "He needs a good woman like you."

"Grandma…" His ears reddened, making Trish grin.

CHAPTER TWELVE

*E*ric stood on the sidewalk on Dauphine Street outside Natasha's hair salon, clutching his ancestor's journal in both hands and watching the people passing by. A violinist stood on the corner, playing a cover of a popular rock song, and tourists gathered around to listen in the summer heat.

He'd slept fitfully last night, checking the clock nearly every hour and hoping Trish would be okay. She had insisted on staying in the house alone, assuring him she believed what his grandmother had said about the curse only affecting Thompson women. But Eric wasn't so sure. Call it a hunch or paranoia; either way, his concern for her safety had him lying awake most of the night.

Thankfully, Natasha had time to look at the journal this afternoon between appointments. He would rest a lot easier if she could confirm his grandmother's statement.

Trish approached from across the street, her red dress swishing around her knees as she paced toward him. She wore black sandals, and she'd pinned a black flower on one side of her hair.

Absolutely stunning. He reminded himself to breathe.

She stepped onto the sidewalk and adjusted her purse strap on her shoulder. "Hey. Thanks for waiting. The meeting with the interior designer took longer than I expected."

"No worries. You're right on time. Did you sleep okay last night?"

She shrugged and looked over her shoulder before rubbing the back of her neck. "Still having the nightmares, but I'm glad to know it's just my imagination. I checked an ancestry website my cousin put together this morning, and I couldn't find any mention of a Thompson in my lineage."

"That's good to know. I'll feel better if Natasha can get rid of the curse, though."

"Yeah, me too. It would be awful if one of their relatives happened to visit New Orleans and stayed at the house." She looked over her left shoulder again and jerked her head to the right.

"Everything okay?" He peered behind her and down the street. Other than the usual people milling about, nothing seemed out of the ordinary.

"Fine. I kept feeling like someone was following me on my way here, but I'm sure it's nothing. I forget how much attention this dress draws, a lot of people noticing me."

"It does look good on you." Though, he'd notice her no matter what she wore.

"Thanks. Should we go in?"

"After you." He opened the door and followed her inside.

Three hairstylists had clients in their chairs, and Natasha pressed her foot on a lever, lowering her customer so she could exit. "Be with you in a second."

Trish sat in the waiting area and patted the chair next to her for Eric to sit. "I love the way hair salons smell, especially when someone is getting their hair colored. Is that weird?"

He inhaled deeply and wrinkled his nose. "Smells like ammonia to me."

"That and shampoos and hair products." She toyed with the hem of her dress. "My mom passed away when I was twelve, but she used to take me to the hair salon with her once a month when she had her roots done. There was a junior stylist who would do my hair in these elaborate French braids while I waited." She looked at him and smiled sadly.

"I can see why you love the smell."

"Come on to the break room, and I'll take a look at your book." Natasha gestured for them to follow her.

They stood, and Eric instinctively rested a hand on the small of Trish's back as they walked through the salon. When they reached the break room, Natasha pulled out two chairs before sinking into a third. Eric slid the journal toward her, opening it to the bookmarked page.

"Mrs. Landry reads French," Trish said. "She offered to translate it, but we figured you'd want to read it in its original form."

"You figured right." She set a pair of glasses on her nose and peered at the book.

"She told us the curse only affected Thompson women." Trish drummed her fingers on the table, and Eric rested a hand on top of hers, both to comfort her and to give Natasha a moment to read in peace.

"Mm-hmm…" Natasha's brows crept toward her hairline as she scanned the journal entry. She shook her head and turned the page, blinking as if she couldn't believe what it said.

"Did my grandma misinterpret it?" Eric asked.

The priestess held up a finger, her gaze never straying from the book. She turned another page, then another, before finally flipping back to the beginning of the entry and letting out a slow breath. She set the book aside and laid her hands palms up on the table. "Let me see your hands," she said to Trish, who swallowed hard and glanced at Eric.

"What did the journal say?" he asked again.

"I need to see your hands, child."

"Okay..." Trish placed her hands in Natasha's, and the priestess closed her eyes. Trish gave him a questioning look, and he shook his head. He had no idea what she was doing.

Natasha swayed slightly, and the energy in the room thickened. Eric had learned his lesson, though, and he didn't dare reach out to see what the priestess might be feeling. She whispered something under her breath, and Trish tensed, her eyes growing wide in alarm, so Eric rested his hand on her back, rubbing circles between her shoulder blades.

"Don't touch her." Natasha opened one eye. "You're contaminating her energy."

"Sorry." He moved his hand to his lap and waited, his gaze darting around the room faster than his knee bounced beneath the table. The break room held a microwave, a small fridge, and a sink. A washing machine and dryer lined the far wall, and a set of towels tumbled behind the glass door.

Natasha finally released her hold of Trish and slid the journal back in front of her. "Your ancestor Delphine didn't understand what she was asking. The spell she had Phillis cast cursed any woman in charge of the house. It ain't specific to the family."

Trish gasped and touched her fingers to her lips.

Eric's heart sank. "So Trish isn't safe in the house."

"Trish ain't safe anywhere. It already took hold of her." She scanned the journal page again.

"How do I stop it? Can you make me a potion or do an exorcism or something?" Tears gathered on her lower lids.

Natasha shook her head. "Curses don't work that way."

"What if she moves out? If she isn't the lady of the house anymore, will the magic wear off?"

"I don't want to move out." Trish wiped beneath her eyes. "I want to fight it. That house is my dream."

"Curses don't work that way either." Natasha closed the book and handed it to Eric. "This hex affects the mind slowly. You'll hear whispers, see things that aren't there, have nightmares. You'll have moments of panic...what they would have called hysteria back then...and then periods of relief where everything feels normal."

A whimper emanated from Trish's throat. "It's already happening."

The priestess folded her arms on the table. "Keep in mind times are different now. A woman could be locked up at her first hysterical episode back then, and that would only make the problem worse. You've got some good friends who'll help you, plenty of time to fight it."

"What do you suggest we do?" Eric asked.

"Since she hasn't been there long, there's a small..." She shook her head. "There's a tiny chance it would wear off over time if she moved far away, but there's only one sure-fire way to end the curse for good."

"I'll do it." Trish straightened and rested her hands on the table. "Whatever it is, I'll do it. I'm staying in the house."

"How do we stop it?" he asked.

Natasha looked first at Trish and then at Eric. "You have to make Trish a Landry."

"What?" She balked like it was the most awful idea she'd ever heard.

Ouch. Eric cleared his throat. "Do you mean change her last name?"

Natasha lifted a brow. "You know exactly what I mean. The curse will end when the lady of the house is married to a Landry. You two already have a strong connection. It's time you acted on it."

"We can't get married, Eric." Trish's stomach twisted in knots as they walked down Dumaine toward Frenchmen Street. The sun warmed the top of her head, but icy tendrils of dread crept through her chest and down her limbs.

"Not even to end a curse? To save your life?" If he was trying to hide the hurt in his eyes, he was doing a terrible job.

She slowed her pace and rubbed her arms, trying to chase away the skin-crawling sensation that reached down into her muscles. Her shoulder hitched upward, and an electrical feeling burned through her veins. "It's nothing personal."

"It feels personal." He shook his head. "Let's be rational about this before we throw out any ideas, okay? Have you had lunch?"

"I'm too emotional to eat."

"I think better on a full stomach. Come at least sit with me so we can talk it through."

"Yeah. Okay." Eric did have a way of calming her down. At the very least, the pounding in her temples might ease.

"Come on." He rested his hand on her back, and his touch immediately took the edge off her nerves. *Think rationally.* She could do that.

She walked by his side until the bright blue building with yellow shutters and a pink wrought-iron gallery came into view. Dat Dog had been the Ghost Tours crew's go-to restaurant for as long as Trish had known them, and the moment she walked in the door and smelled the delicious scents of a dozen different types of sausages on the grill, her stomach growled.

Eric ordered a Chicago-style hot dog before looking at her. "You should eat something."

She chewed the inside of her cheek, her hunger battling with her nausea for control of her stomach. "I'll just have a Dr Pepper and some fries…with cheese, bacon, and ranch."

They took their drinks to a quiet room upstairs, and Eric folded his arms on the table. "Before you completely dismiss the idea, I am willing to marry you if it means breaking a centuries-long curse and saving your sanity."

"Of course you are. A Landry always gets what he wants." Her tone was sharper than she intended, and the look in his eyes said the jab had hurt.

"I wanted to date you, not marry you." He scoffed, recovering. "Having a wife is the furthest thing from my mind."

Now it was her turn to feel the sting. "Your grandma

seemed intent on playing matchmaker. You don't think she invited me into the house knowing that—"

"No." He shook his head adamantly. "She's pushy and persistent, but she would never do something like that."

She pursed her lips. Throwing out accusations wouldn't help the situation, and honestly, she didn't believe what she'd insinuated. Not for a minute. "You're right. My mind is going all over the place right now. I don't know why that popped into my brain and slid out of my mouth." Probably because the idea of marrying Eric didn't sound nearly as awful as it should have, and that terrified her.

A server delivered their food, and Trish toyed with a plastic fork while Eric bit into his hotdog. She'd offended him. Eric was the sweetest, most generous man she knew, and she'd accused him and his grandmother of cursing her so she'd have to marry him. What was wrong with her?

She shoved a cheesy, ranchy, bacony fry into her mouth and stared out the window. She needed to apologize, to explain it wasn't *him* who was the problem, but she couldn't find the words.

"You weren't hungry at all, were you?" Eric's voice pulled her from her thoughts, and she looked down to find she'd polished off her entire plate of fries.

"You always know exactly what I need." She sipped her drink. "I'm really sorry for saying that about your grandma. I don't think y'all orchestrated this to force me to marry you."

"I would never make you do something you didn't want to do."

"I know. You're a good friend, Eric, and I can think of a lot worse men to be married to." Hell, with the way her love life was going, this would probably be her only chance at matrimony. And it wasn't like she had to *stay* married to him. Nowadays, marriages were rarely forever anyway.

"Is that a yes, then? Will you marry me?" He swallowed hard as if the words affected him more than he expected them to.

"You're not down on one knee with a ring in your hand, but if it'll save my sanity, let's do it." She held his gaze, and her blood felt fizzy in her veins while her head spun in an oddly pleasant way. She was going to marry Eric. *Holy crap.*

"I can get you a ring." He pressed the straw to his lips and lowered his gaze.

"There's umm… Don't do that. It's not a real marriage." This was probably one of her snap decisions that would end badly, but what else could she do? The *tiny* chance that moving out might make the magic wear off wasn't worth the risk. Not at the rate her mind was spiraling downward.

"Natasha said you have to marry a Landry. I don't think a pretend ceremony is going to cut it. We'll need to get a license, make it official."

"Right, but we're doing it to break the curse, and then we'll get it annulled. You can get an annulment in Louisiana, can't you?"

"I think so." He pulled out his phone and typed on the screen before nodding. "It seems like a straightforward process."

"Perfect." *Oof.* A wave of nausea washed through her, and she pressed her fingers to her lips. *You practically inhaled a massive order of gooey fries, Trish. What do you expect?*

"Are you okay?"

"Yeah. Just ate too fast." She sipped her drink to settle her stomach. "Are you busy this afternoon? We might as well do it now. Why waste another day?"

He froze with a deer-in-the-headlights expression for a moment before he composed himself. "Yeah. The office is downtown. It says we'll need our IDs and birth certificates."

"Mine's at the house."

"Mine too."

"Meet you there, and then we'll drive to the office together?" Her right shoulder pulled up toward her ear as the prickling, skin-crawling sensation made her muscles tense. She rubbed the back of her neck and shook her head to chase away the high-pitched ringing in her ears. This marriage couldn't happen fast enough.

"Are you okay to drive? I can call Jason and ask him to take your car home."

"I'm fine. I just want to end this curse before it gets its claws into me any deeper."

He gave her a skeptical look, and she held his gaze, arching a brow. Finally, he relented. "Okay. I'll see you at the house."

Trish walked three blocks to the parking lot, climbed into her Toyota, and headed to the Garden District. Her stomach roiled, the nauseating cocktail consisting of equal parts excitement that she could beat this, nervousness that she had to marry Eric to do it, and dread that it would all fall apart. The solution seemed way too simple.

Her pulse thrummed, and she tapped her fingers on the steering wheel. The air in the car felt heavy, thick, and she cranked up the AC to combat the suffocating sensation. She was doing the right thing. She only had two options: move out, give up her dream, and cross her fingers that the curse would lose potency over time or marry the man who was becoming one of her closest friends and end the curse for good.

It was a no-brainer. So why did she have such an overwhelming feeling of impending doom? It was her anxiety getting the better of her. She needed to take a deep breath and chill before she— "Ahh!"

She slammed on the brakes, holding the steering wheel in a death grip as her car skidded to a stop inches from the one in front of her. She dropped her head back against the headrest and closed her eyes. *Get it together, girl.* She had to get out of her mind and into the moment, or she wouldn't make it back to the house at all.

A horn blared from behind her, and she opened her eyes to find the light had turned green, the car she narrowly missed slamming into long gone. She waved at the car behind her, fighting the urge to give them the one-fingered salute, and drove to the house to get her birth certificate.

"Eric, are you in here?" The front door squeaked on its hinges as she pushed it open, which didn't help the anxiety attack she was trying to subdue. "Luke?" The contractors must have been on their lunch break because the house was eerily quiet.

She darted up the stairs to her bedroom, grabbed her birth certificate from the file box, and raced back down with her heart in her throat.

"Are you sure you're okay?" Eric's voice gave her fright, and her foot slipped on the step. She caught the railing before she took a tumble, but good gravy. Her mind was getting out of control. She dropped onto a step and held her head in her hands.

"Hey." Eric sat beside her and rubbed her back. "What's going on?"

"It's my anxiety. I almost rear-ended someone on my way here, and I... I need a breather." She leaned into him, letting his warmth and gentle touch soothe her frazzled nerves.

"We can wait. Do you want to think about it for a few days? Maybe we can find another Voodoo practitioner to look at the curse. We can get a second opinion."

"No." She lifted her head. "I want to do this. I trust Natasha."

He checked the time on his phone. "They close in an hour."

"We better get going then." She hauled herself up and walked with Eric out the door.

Her anxiety eased on the drive. Something about being near him, his calm demeanor, his level-headed way of thinking, grounded her. He didn't judge her when she freaked out. He was patient and kind, and she should have become better friends with him a long time ago.

By the time they reached the office, her anxiety had vanished, and she smiled as they stepped up to the counter. "We'd like to get a marriage license, please."

She filled out the form, and, after they both signed it, they passed their documents to the clerk. Eric's jaw was tight, and he drummed his fingers against his thigh as the woman processed their request. He paid the fee, and the woman set their license on the counter. Neither of them touched it.

"Where do we go to make it official?" Trish asked.

"The parish courthouse, but there's a twenty-four-hour waiting period."

"Seriously?" Trish grabbed the license and the rest of

their papers, tapping them on the counter to even the stack. "You should have that information on your website."

"We do." She forced a smile.

"Eric?"

He held up his hands. "It was a last-minute decision. I just skimmed the website."

"Which is exactly why we have the waiting period," the woman said. "Go home and think about it. Marriage is a big step, and a divorce is much harder—and more expensive—to obtain."

"We won't be getting a divorce." Trish turned and strode out of the office.

When they reached Eric's car, he opened her door and she climbed inside. "Listen," he said as he slid into the driver's seat. "I don't think you should stay in the house tonight. I know Natasha said the curse will follow you, but I'll feel a lot better if you're not alone."

"After the day I've had, I think you're right. I'll call Emily and see if I can stay with her."

He nodded. "I'll drive you there."

"You don't have to do that."

"I want to. Let me take care of you until this curse is broken. I am your fiancé, after all." He winked and started the car.

"Thank you, Eric."

"I'm going to be the best husband you've ever had."

She laughed. "You'll be the only husband I've ever had.

"With the bar that low, there's no way I can fail."

CHAPTER THIRTEEN

"My god, Trish. I don't even know what to say." Emily sat on the edge of the bed next to her in the guest room. After swinging by the house to get some clothes, Eric had driven her straight to her friend's house for the night.

"It's par for my life, though, isn't it?" She smoothed the comforter and stared at her toes. The hot pink polish had started to chip. "I finally get control of my finances and feel like my life is beginning, and I get hit with a curse that's going to drive me insane. Everything I do turns into disaster."

"But you always manage. Life has thrown you an orchard of lemons."

She laughed dryly. "I have gotten good at making lemonade, haven't I?"

"You're the best." Emily cut her gaze toward the door as Sable let out an irritated wail.

"We're fine," Sean called from down the hall. "She dropped her binkie."

"You've got yourself a good one," Trish said.

"I know. So, you and Eric, huh? Who knew marrying the man of your dreams would solve all your problems?" Emily elbowed her side playfully.

She rolled her eyes. "He is not the man of my dreams... My wet dreams, maybe."

"Have y'all done anything?"

"No!" She pulled her knees to her chest, wrapping her arms around her legs. "We've been keeping things professional. We're friends. That's all."

"Friends who are about to get married."

"To break a curse."

"Is that the only reason?"

"What are you implying, Em? That I'm secretly in love with him, and I'm not telling you? If I fell in love with anyone, you would be the first to know."

"I would, wouldn't I?"

Trish scoffed. "You're impossible. We are getting married purely to break the curse. Once that's done, we'll get an annulment and things will go back to the way they were. It's what we both want."

"If you say so."

"What other choice do I have? Sure, I could move out, and it might help, but the curse would still be there. If another woman moved in to run the B and B, she'd be cursed too. I can't let that happen."

"She wouldn't be cursed if she married Eric. Maybe one of his old girlfriends could marry him and move in for a while. He's quite a catch." Emily arched a brow as if gauging Trish's reaction.

She tried to keep a neutral expression, but she'd be lying if she said the idea of him being with another woman didn't give her a pang of jealousy, which was utterly ridiculous. They were just friends. He could have a wife, and it wouldn't change their relationship.

Emily tucked one leg beneath her other. "When you make that face, your emotions are so obvious."

"What emotions?"

"Don't play dumb."

"Fine. I don't want anyone else to marry him, okay? But this isn't how I wanted my first—and hopefully only—marriage to go." She sat criss-cross and faced her friend. "I thought I would be married with kids by now, but the man I thought I'd spend forever with turned out to be an ass. Actually, that's not fair. I was the ass for following him out here, but that doesn't change my fantasy of having a beautiful wedding with a gown and flowers and everything."

"A wedding is just one day."

"Our marriage won't last much longer."

"It could."

"It can't. I won't have the reason I spend the rest of my life with someone be because some rich old lady was mad at her husband for gambling too much."

Sean knocked on the open door. "Sable's bathed and ready for bed."

"On my way." Emily patted Trish's knee before standing. "You're doing the right thing."

"Will you come tomorrow? For moral support?"

"Of course."

Trish spent the evening watching *Golden Girls* reruns with her friends, but the light-hearted comedy didn't ease the anxiety slowly creeping back into her system. She only ate one slice of the pizza they ordered, which was so unlike her. Pepperoni and bacon were her favorites.

She wanted to turn in early, but the nightmares she'd

been having made her hesitate. "I'd ask for some salt, but it didn't help me at home."

"We keep the entire property salted," Sean said. "With two mediums under the same roof, we're like a lighthouse for the dead."

"I'm sure you'll sleep better," Emily said. "We're just a few feet away if you need us."

"Thanks."

Exhaustion dragged her under shortly after her head hit the pillow, but the change in sleeping arrangements didn't quell the terrifying dreams. Panic coursed through her veins as the same invisible force held her down, but this time Eric was there too. He stood in the corner of the room, watching as she thrashed against her restraints.

"Eric!" she shouted in her dream. "Help me!"

He shook his head and walked away, and her heart wrenched in her chest. On her feet again, she found herself inside the box, but rather than clawing at the wood to get out, she leaned her head against the splintered surface and cried.

"Trish?" Emily's voice sounded somewhere in the distance, but she didn't bother opening her eyes. What was the point?

"Trish, wake up." A hand on her shoulder gave her a shake, and she sucked in a breath. The air smelled of lavender, not dirt and decay, so she blinked open her eyes.

"Em?" She tried to sit up, but the sheets were in a tangle.

Her friend helped unknot her. "You were sobbing in your sleep."

"Ugh." She rubbed her eyes. "These nightmares will be the death of me."

"Don't say that."

"It's the truth. One of these days, I'll have a heart attack in my sleep." She shook her head. That was an unpleasant thought. "What time is it?"

"Ten. You've been asleep for twelve hours."

Yet she felt like she hadn't slept in days. "Sorry."

"Don't be. You needed it." Emily climbed onto the bed next to her. "What time is your appointment?"

"Four. Eric's picking me up at three."

"No, he's not. I'm taking you." She patted her leg. "Now, get up. We've got a lot to do."

Trish groaned. "Like what?"

"First, we're going to brunch. Then we're getting our nails done and buying you something to wear."

She rubbed her forehead. "I'm really not in the mood."

"Get your ass out of bed, woman. I'm not letting you spend the afternoon sulking. It's your wedding day."

Emily's words might have made her smile a little. Okay, a lot.

"Damn, Eric." Jason set his beer on the table and leaned his elbow on the gallery railing. "I knew you had it bad for Trish, but cursing her to convince her to marry you?"

"I didn't curse her." Eric took a swig of Abita and stared out at the crowd meandering through Jackson Square. A fan whirled the sticky summer air into a bearable temperature, but most people kept to the air-conditioned inside of restaurants this time of year, so they had the gallery to themselves.

"I know." Jason grinned. "I'm just giving you a hard time."

"Don't joke like that in front of her. She already

accused my grandma and me of concocting a scheme to make her my wife." His voice cracked on the last word, and he tried to hide his reaction by taking another drink.

"Ouch."

"Tell me about it."

"But she's cool with it now?"

He shrugged. "I guess. She doesn't believe we tricked her, so that's a plus."

"Do you think it'll work?"

He took a deep breath and wiped the condensation from his mug. "Natasha read the curse and said the only way to stop it was to make Trish a Landry, so yeah. She hasn't steered any of us wrong yet."

Jason nodded thoughtfully. "At least your grandma will stop trying to set you up."

"Doubtful. Once we get it annulled, I'm sure she'll be back at it in full force."

Jason narrowed his eyes skeptically. "You really think you'll get it annulled? Is that what you want?"

He opened his mouth to say it was what they both wanted, but the words wouldn't pass his lips. All he'd thought about since this whole ordeal began was Trish. He loved having her in the house, seeing her every day. He adored everything about her. "It's what she wants."

"Is it?"

"She said she does."

Jason laughed. "Women don't always say what they mean. You know that."

"Better than anyone."

"But for the first time, you can't tell what the woman wants, regardless of what she says."

Eric slumped in his seat. "I don't have a clue."

"Welcome to the world the rest of us live in."

"How do you cope with being so clueless all the time?"

"You're not as clueless as you think. You've been relying on a crutch that's useless around Trish, but you've got enough experience with women to figure her out."

Eric returned his gaze to Jackson Square. A couple bought ice cream from a vendor's cart and sat on a bench facing the St. Louis Cathedral. His grandparents were married in the enormous eighteenth-century church before having a second-line parade through the streets of the French Quarter on their way to the reception. Now, Eric was about to head to the courthouse to marry the woman of his dreams with the intent of ending it as soon as possible.

"She deserves better."

"C'mon, man. Don't sell yourself short." Jason leaned his forearms on the table. "Is she still ragging on you about your age?"

He shook his head. "She said it was a defense mechanism."

"Defense against what?"

"Us becoming more than friends."

"Well, there you go. You know how she feels, so make your fake marriage real."

"Sure." He'd have to be delusional to pretend what he and Trish were about to do was real. She'd made it clear she wanted out as soon as possible. "I'm going to stop by my grandma's and let her know what's going on before heading to the courthouse to meet Trish. Will you be there?"

"You know it. I wouldn't miss seeing the two people I never thought I'd see tied down get tied to each other."

Eric paid the tab and navigated the narrow streets of the French Quarter. With so many pedestrians wandering about and service trucks taking up most of the road as they parked and made their deliveries, driving here was next to impossible. He kept telling himself he should park in a paid lot in the Central Business District and walk, but the heat and humidity made grabbing a spot at Ghost Tours HQ in the center of the French Quarter far too tempting.

Speaking of tempting… An image of Trish in her pajama shorts and tank top flashed through his mind as he crossed Canal Street and made his way into the CBD. Taller, more modern brick structures replaced the quaint nineteenth-century wooden buildings, but he hardly noticed the view. He drove almost on autopilot as Jason's words rolled around in his mind. *Make the fake marriage real.*

The idea intrigued him; there was no denying that.

He reached his grandma's estate and hit the remote, and the black cast-iron gate blocking the driveway rolled aside. He found her inside the parlor, chatting with a guest, and when he stopped in the doorway, she gestured for him to enter.

"This is the grandson I was telling you about. Isn't he handsome?"

"He sure is." The guest smiled and shook his hand.

"If things don't work with you and Trish, Gladys has a beautiful granddaughter."

"She would adore you," Gladys said.

Eric chuckled and clutched his ancestor's journal to his chest. "Speaking of Trish. Could I talk to you privately for a minute?"

"I'll get out of your hair. It was a pleasure to meet you, young man." Gladys shuffled out of the room.

"There are more guests in the dining room," his

grandma said. "If this is about what's in that book, we should go to my bedroom."

"Lead the way." He followed her up the stairs and into her suite before closing the door and setting the book on a table near the window. "The curse has ahold of Trish."

Her brows disappeared into her hair. "She's a Thompson after all?"

"No, Grandma. That curse wasn't specific to the family. It affects *any* woman who runs the house."

"I see." She sank into a chair. "I had no idea."

"I believe you, but Trish is already showing symptoms. If we don't do something fast, she's going to succumb to the same fate as every other lady of the house since Phillis cast her spell."

"What can I do?"

"You just have to understand. Trish and I are getting married this afternoon at the courthouse. The only way to break the curse is to make her part of the family."

She looked up at him and smiled. "Well, that's good news, isn't it? You end the hex *and* get your girl. It sounds like fate if you ask me."

He shook his head and sat in the chair next to her. "We're getting it annulled as soon as the curse is lifted. I just wanted you to hear it from me in case someone you know sees us."

"Mm-hmm." She narrowed her eyes and puckered her lips.

"I don't need a lecture about this. She's not in love with me, so it will be annulled."

"Do you at least have a ring for her?"

"It's not a real marriage."

"For the days that it lasts, it most certainly is." She rose and walked to the closet. A box sliding across a shelf sounded from inside before she grunted. "Come in here and help your grandmother. I can't reach it."

He strode to the closet and found her on her toes, stretching toward the top shelf. He grabbed the small cedar box in question and handed it to her.

"If you can wait a few days, I'd love to plan a real wedding for you. We could do it here at the house. Anything would be better than the courthouse."

"Even if there was time to wait, it wouldn't matter. We don't want to make a big deal out of something temporary."

"At least use these." She scooped two rings out of the box and placed them in his hand. "These belonged to your granddad's parents."

His pulse kicked up as he stared at the gold bands in his palm. His great-grandmother's ring had a large rectangular diamond in the center with two small ones on either side. This sure would make his fake wedding feel real. "This isn't necessary."

"I insist. *If* you choose to end the marriage, I trust Trish will return the ring."

As if the choice was his alone. "It's not a real—"

"Please take them. They were supposed to go to your mother if she ever got married, but we both know they'd end up in a pawn shop if she got her hands on them."

He folded his fingers around the rings. "We'll take good care of them."

"I know. What time should I be at the courthouse?"

"You don't have to come."

She pushed her glasses up her nose and gave him the same stern look that always stopped him in his tracks as a kid. She didn't have to say a word to get her message across.

"Four o'clock."

She raked her gaze over him. "You are going home to shower and change."

"Yeah. I'll clean myself up."

"Wear something nice. Slacks and a jacket this time. No jeans."

He chuckled and walked toward the hallway. "Yes, ma'am."

"And Eric?"

He paused and turned toward her.

"I don't expect to get those rings back."

CHAPTER FOURTEEN

"I still think this is going overboard." Trish climbed out of Emily's car and stepped onto the sidewalk in front of the courthouse. "Eric's probably wearing the same jeans and t-shirt he's had on all day."

"I doubt that." Emily closed her door and moved toward the entrance. "You look absolutely beautiful, as you should on your wedding day."

Nausea rolled through her stomach, and she swallowed the bitter taste creeping up the back of her throat. Emily had taken her to get both her hair and nails done that morning. Then, she'd insisted on buying Trish a new outfit to wear to this sham of a wedding.

The knee-length champagne dress had a layer of lace over satin with a halter-style, racerback top. It was gorgeous but way too dressy for the occasion.

"The only reason I agreed to all this is that today might be the only wedding I ever have."

"Which is why you should enjoy yourself, even if it's just pretend." She stopped outside the courthouse door. "I still think you should have let the rest of the crew come. They'd have loved to be here for you."

"No. Absolutely not. I don't want to give this any more meaning than it has to have." Because if she got swept up in it, she might forget the reason Eric proposed. It wasn't because they expected to live happily ever after together. He was doing her a favor. Nothing more.

"It's going to break a curse and save your sanity. I'd say that means a lot." Emily opened the door and stepped aside. "After you, bestie."

With a deep inhale, Trish straightened her spine and walked through the door. The courthouse bustled with activity—if you could call waiting in line and filling out forms activity. She and Emily followed the signs to their assigned room and found Eric, his grandmother, and Jason sitting in the chairs outside the door. So much for not making this out to mean more than it should.

He shot to his feet the moment his eyes met hers, and the familiar flutter in her belly rose to her chest. He looked scrumptious in dark pants with a matching jacket, and his cream-colored shirt had the top two buttons undone.

"Did you tell him to dress up?" she whispered out of the side of her mouth as he approached.

"I only told him I'd be bringing you here," Emily said. "The rest is all Eric."

"Hi, Trish." He let his gaze wander down her body before returning to her eyes. "You look stunning."

"Thanks. You look nice too." Heat rose to her cheeks. "Why did you bring an audience?"

"You've got a maid of honor. It's only fair that I get a best man." His smile was forced as if he were nervous. At least she wasn't the only one.

"What about your grandma?"

He splayed his hands. "I couldn't stop her."

The courtroom door opened, and a couple walked out arm in arm. The woman had to be at least eight months pregnant, and the man rested his hand on her basketball of a belly as they thanked the woman standing there with a clipboard.

"Eric Landry and Trish Bennett?" She tilted her head expectantly, and Trish swallowed hard.

"That's us." Eric looked at Trish and smiled, but she couldn't return the gesture.

She crossed one arm over her chest, her fingers drumming rapidly against her collar bone against her will. Her throat closed up until she felt like she was breathing through a cocktail stirrer. She swayed on her feet, her lungs refusing to draw in air, and the overwhelming urge to vomit had her eyes rolling back and her lids fluttering shut.

"Trish?" Eric's voice was a distant echo.

"I've got her." That was Emily, she thought, but she couldn't be sure. "Right over here." A gentle touch on her elbow guided her to a chair. "Lean forward. Head between your knees."

Trish did as she was told. Anything to make the room stop spinning and brunch stay in her stomach where it belonged.

"What's happening to her? Is it the curse?" Eric whispered the last part.

"She's having an anxiety attack." Emily sat next to her and rubbed her back. "You're okay. Take a deep breath."

She filled her lungs with the biggest breath her posture would allow, but it didn't stop her body from trembling. Sweat beaded on her forehead. *Fantastic.* She went to all this trouble to look nice for Eric, and now her stupid anxiety was ruining it. She dragged in a ragged breath.

"Are you sure?" Eric asked.

"I've seen it before."

"With her or with your patients?"

"Both. She'll be fine. Just give her a minute."

She cleared the thickness from her throat. "Stop talking about me like I'm not here."

"Trish." Eric sat on her other side and rested his hand on her back. "If you don't want to do this, we can leave. We can try to find another way."

"No." She sucked in another breath and lifted her head.

Eric's gaze was filled with concern, and he kneeled in front of her, taking her hands in his. "Tell me what you want to do." His touch soothed her, and she finally caught her breath.

"I want to do this. We have to." She sat up straight, testing her equilibrium. The room had finally stopped spinning.

"Are you sure?"

"Yeah." She rose, tugging him up with her, and she was steady on her feet. "I'm okay. My body sometimes reacts before my brain can even catch up." She looked at the clerk waiting at the door. "I'm sorry."

The woman smiled. "No worries, dear. It happens all the time, though it's usually the men on the verge of passing out. Are you ready now?"

"We're ready." A swarm of butterflies took flight in her stomach as she linked her arm around Eric's and walked with him down the aisle. Well, it wasn't much of an aisle. There were a few rows of benches and a judge waiting for them on the other side of the room, but it was close enough to keep her insides tied in knots and her pulse pounding in her ears. She tightened her grip on Eric's arm to keep herself steady, and he gave her a questioning look similar to the one he gave her that fateful day when her date to his murder mystery show turned out to be a narcissistic ass.

Was she okay? She either felt sick from the curse or her nerves. If it was the former, all the more reason to get this over with. If it was her nerves, well, she just needed to get over *herself*.

As their friends sat in the front row, the judge looked from Eric to Trish. "Shall we begin?"

She nodded, and he launched into the "we are gathered here today" speech. She barely heard a word of it. This felt so wrong, but not for the reason she expected. She liked Eric. A lot. And her feelings for him had grown from purely physical to something much deeper. The intention behind this ceremony was to end the marriage ASAP, and *that* was what felt wrong.

"Eric," the judge said, "do you take this woman to be your wife, to live together in matrimony, to love, honor, and comfort her, and to hold her in sickness and in health for as long as you both shall live?"

Eric's eyes widened like a deer in the headlights. He didn't blink. Didn't move.

"Eric?" the judge asked again.

He swallowed hard and looked at Trish. "I do," he lied.

"Do you have rings?"

Trish shook her head. "No, we don't have—"

Eric tugged something from his pocket and grasped her left hand. She couldn't bring herself to look as the cool metal band slid onto her finger.

"What are you doing?" she whispered. "You weren't supposed to buy me a ring."

"I didn't."

She glanced down at the massive rectangular diamond in an art deco setting. *Holy crap.* This looked like a family heirloom. *Breathe, Trish. Do not pass out now.* She unlocked her knees to avoid the fate of so many grooms in the funny wedding videos she'd seen on TV.

"Trish…" the judge continued. "Do you take this man to be your husband…"

Oh, crap. It was her turn to lie. Her bejeweled hands trembled, so she clenched her fists. *In through the nose, out through the mouth.* She could do this.

"…for as long as you both shall live?"

She forced the words over her thickening throat. "I do."

Eric held up a golden band, and she took it. His hand was warm, and her heart beat a million miles a minute as she slid the ring onto his finger. She blew out a breath and looked into his eyes. His expression had softened, a look of something akin to adoration sparking in his gaze. He smiled softly, and the knot her stomach had tied itself into released, a flood of warmth running through her veins and flushing the anxiety from her system.

They'd done it. They'd said their "I do's," and now she was married to the hottest, sweetest, most generous man she'd ever met. *This isn't so bad, is it?*

"By the power vested in me by the state of Louisiana, it is my honor to declare you married. You may seal this declaration with a kiss."

Oh, boy.

"Want to make it official?" Eric winked.

"Why not?" She leaned in and brushed her lips to his.

Her plan was to give him a quick peck on his mouth and pull away, but when she got that close to the man she'd had the hots for all these years, she didn't have a chance. His lips were soft, contrasting with the coarse hair of his beard. He smelled warm like spice, and her legs moved before the action registered in her brain.

Her body pressed to his, she slid her arms around his shoulders and kissed him like she meant it. An *mmm* vibrated from his throat, so quiet it would have been imperceptible to the rest of the room. Like it was meant for only her.

He wrapped his arms around her waist, holding her closer before sliding one hand up to cradle the back of her head. She parted her lips, and he accepted the invitation, slipping out his tongue to brush against hers. Warmth unfurled in her chest and rolled down below her navel.

He tasted like wintergreen, the coolness of the mint opposing the heat of...well, of everything else about him. She tightened her arms around him. Why hadn't she done this a long time ago?

"Congratulations," the judge said.

Trish gasped as Eric broke the kiss, and she stood there stunned, unable to remember a single reason why she'd refused his advances all these years.

"You did it." Emily patted her back, breaking the spell Eric's kiss had put her under.

"Hearts are shattering tonight," Jason said. "New Orleans' most eligible bachelor is off the market."

Hopefully her heart wouldn't be next.

"Welcome to the family, Trish." Eric's grandma hugged her.

"Thank you, Mrs. Landry."

"You can call me Betty, dear. You're family."

They signed the documents and filed out of the courthouse before gathering in the parking lot.

Emily retrieved Trish's overnight bag from her backseat and offered it to her. "I assume you're going home with Eric?"

"Yeah. We need to convince the house we're married, I think." She reached for the bag, but Eric grabbed it and slung it over his shoulder.

"That's it?" Jason tugged his keys from his pocket. "The curse is broken?"

"I hope so," Trish said.

"Is Natasha coming out to check?" Emily asked.

"She's out of town," Eric said. "I called her this morning. She'll be in Missouri visiting a sick cousin for a week, but she said we'd know within a day or two if it worked."

"Everyone, keep your fingers and toes crossed." Trish took off the ring and offered it to Eric, but Betty stopped her with a hand on her arm.

"As long as you're married to Eric, that ring is yours."

"But it'll only be a few days."

"Then it's yours for a few days. You can return it if you go through with the annulment."

She put it back on. There was no sense in arguing. "I'm exhausted. Do you mind if we head home?"

"Call me if you need anything." Emily gave her a quick hug, and Eric opened the passenger door for her.

"How are you feeling?" he asked as he slid into the driver's seat.

Good question. "I'm okay. A lot of emotions whirling around, so I can't tell if the curse is broken."

"You nearly passed out in there." He pulled out of the parking lot and headed toward the Garden District.

"My anxiety got the better of me. It happens more

often than I care to admit. Thanks for being patient with me."

"Thanks for kissing me."

She laughed. "Was it everything you hoped it would be?"

"Better."

On that, they could agree.

They arrived at the mansion, and Eric took her bag from the back seat before walking with her to the porch. Trish unlocked the door, but before she could step inside, he clutched her arm.

"Hold on. We have to make this look real, right?" Before she could answer, he moved his arm beneath her knees, literally sweeping her off her feet, and he carried her across the threshold.

She couldn't fight her smile as he lowered her to the ground. She held onto him for a beat longer than necessary, her gaze drifting to his lips, her mind replaying their kiss before he released her and stepped away.

"That should do it." He set her bag on a bench in the foyer. "I guess I'll head to my place."

"Do you want a drink? I've got a bottle of rosé in the fridge."

He cut his gaze toward the door before looking at her. "Sure."

"Don't sound too excited." She paced into the kitchen. "You are married to the woman of your dreams."

"For now." He stared at the annulment form she'd left on the breakfast table, and his jaw tightened. "Got a pen?"

"In a rush?"

"Looks like you are." He sat in the chair in front of the paperwork, his expression pinching like it offended him. "When did you do this?"

"I printed it at Emily's this morning. We stopped by the house to pick up a few things for the ceremony, and I filled it out." She poured the wine and brought a pen to the table before sitting next to him. "Eric, we agreed when we did this that we'd end the marriage as soon as the curse lifted."

He grabbed the pen and signed the document. "You're right. I don't know why I was surprised to see the paperwork already filled out."

"Is something wrong?"

He took a long drink of wine. "A minute ago, you said I was married to the woman of my dreams."

"I was joking. That's kinda our thing, isn't it?"

"Did you notice that I didn't deny it?" He took another drink, watching her over the rim of the glass.

Whoa. "Eric, I don't know what to say."

"Say what you feel."

"I don't… I don't know what I feel." She'd been adamant about not getting involved with him. Her career was at stake, after all. But that kiss changed things. Boy, did it ever. She expected kissing Eric to be hot as sin, but she never counted on it feeling so…right. Like, *where have you been all my life?* right.

But this was what they'd agreed to do. So what if she had the paperwork ready to go? What difference did it make?

He nodded and rose to his feet. "I'll be in my apartment if you need anything."

"I don't understand why you're acting this way."

"I don't either." He turned and walked away.

CHAPTER FIFTEEN

*E*ric lay in bed, staring at the ceiling fan whirring above. What the hell was his problem? What on earth possessed him to act that way?

He knew exactly what.

Kissing Trish at the wedding had been better than he could have ever imagined. And he'd imagined it a lot. He closed his eyes and replayed the moment in his mind. The way she leaned into him, her arms around his shoulders, her lips parting in invitation... She felt something. The sexual desire was there like it always had been, but that kiss felt like more. Like he had a chance.

Then he went and ruined everything when he saw that damn annulment form lying on the table. She had the paperwork filled out before they even said, "I do," and it bothered him more than it should have.

They had agreed on it all. He knew the marriage was going to end from the moment they decided to do it, but his grandma's insistence that it would last and then Trish actually dressing for the occasion had given him the false hope that maybe this could be forever.

That dress… It wasn't exactly a wedding gown, but she looked more beautiful than ever before. And that was no easy feat because she was always gorgeous.

But he knew. He could tell by her posture and the look on her face that when she said, "I do," she really didn't. He knew, but he still pretended she meant it when their kiss sparked fireworks.

He needed to apologize. He had no right to get offended over something like this, and if things were to go back to the way they were before the curse, he needed to march his ass over there and make amends.

He swung his legs over the side of the bed and glanced at the clock. It was one a.m. *Damn.* His apology would have to wait a few hours.

He lay back and folded his hands on his stomach, willing his mind to slow down so he could get a little sleep. But every time he closed his eyes, thoughts of the kiss played like a movie behind his lids.

The tension in his muscles finally began to ease, and just as his body relaxed, a piercing scream reverberated through the windows.

He shot to his feet and darted out the door, running for the main house without a second thought. He twisted the back doorknob and slammed his shoulder against the wood, but it didn't budge. The damn thing was locked, and he'd left his key.

Another shriek echoed from upstairs, and his heart lodged in his throat. "Trish!" He banged the side of his fist against the door.

"Dammit." He ran back to his apartment and grabbed his keys before returning to the mansion and throwing open the door.

"Let her out!" Trish wailed, and he shot up the stairs, taking them two at a time.

She wasn't in the bedroom, so he returned to the hall and followed the sounds of her cries. He found her banging her palm against the disappointments room wall, clawing at the sheetrock as she wept.

"Trish?" He carefully paced toward her, trying his best not to startle her.

"Let her out," she sobbed, her body sagging against the wall.

He gently took her shoulders in his hands and turned her around. "What's going on, *cher*?"

Her eyes were glazed, and as she lifted her gaze to his face, she seemed to look right through him, not focusing on anything. "Trish?" He gave her a gentle shake, and she gasped.

"Eric?" Her body trembled, and she fell against him, clutching his neck. "What's happening? Where…?" She lifted her head and took in her surroundings. When her gaze locked on her claw marks on the wall, she whispered, "Oh my god."

"Come on. Let's get you out of here." With his arms wrapped around her, he guided her through the hallway and into her bedroom.

"I need to sit down," she whispered.

He took her to the bed and sank onto the mattress with her, holding her firmly to his body. She fit in his arms like she belonged there. "I think you were sleepwalking."

"It didn't work, Eric. The nightmares…" She hugged him tightly around the waist, burying her face in his chest. "I'm still cursed."

"Maybe. Maybe not." He stroked her hair. "Nightmares

and sleepwalking can happen to anyone, and stress plays a huge role. You were anxious at the wedding today. Hell, you almost fainted. Maybe tonight's dream was nothing more than your subconscious working through it all."

"Great." She straightened, tugging from his embrace, and wiped beneath her eyes. "I don't need a curse to make me crazy. I'm doing a bang-up job on my own."

"You're not going crazy. You had a stressful day. We both did, and I'm sorry."

"What are you sorry for?"

"For getting offended that you already had the annulment papers filled out. I was out of line, and I apologize."

She nodded, holding his gaze for a long moment, and a magnetism built between them. "That was the first time you've ever acted mad at me." She let her gaze wander down his body, and she moistened her lips. "I didn't like it."

"I'm sorry."

She rested her hand on his thigh, and his stomach tightened. "It made me realize something."

"Oh?" He looked into her eyes, but he couldn't stop his gaze from drifting to her mouth.

She caught her bottom lip between her teeth, hesitating slightly before leaning in and kissing him. Her lips felt like warm velvet, and as she ran her hand up his chest, goosebumps rose on his skin. He gently held her face in his hands and basked in the moment. She smelled like Dove soap and lilacs, like heaven, and when a tiny moan emanated from her throat, his body heated in response.

With one hand on her back, he pulled her closer, deepening the kiss. Her tongue tangled with his as she clutched his shoulders, and, heaven have mercy, she felt good in his arms.

She broke the kiss, trailing her lips down his neck and back up again before nipping his earlobe between her teeth. His goosebumps hardened like pinpricks, and whatever blood was left in his head rushed to his groin.

"I want you, Eric." Her whisper against his ear made his head spin, and as she found his mouth with hers once more, his body shuddered.

How many times had he imagined this moment? Too many to count, for sure, but as much as he wanted to take this as far as she wanted it to go, he couldn't. Not now. Not like this.

"Trish, we can't." It pained him to utter those words. He'd be kicking himself tomorrow for blowing what could be his only chance with her, but he'd feel even worse if they went through with it and she had regrets.

"Why not?" She kissed down his neck and across his collar bone. "We've both wanted this for years. You're already half-naked. It seems such a shame to waste the opportunity."

Such a shame, indeed.

He took her shoulders in his hands and gently pushed her back. "I want you more than you can imagine."

"And I want you to have me." She pinned him with a heated gaze so intense he almost gave in.

God, how he wanted her. *Needed* her. His entire body ached to hold her, to please her, but he shouldn't. "Not this way."

"Not what way?" Her brow crumpled, the sting of rejection causing her to pull away even more.

"The only reason I'm here half-naked is because I heard you scream. You've been adamant for years that nothing will ever happen between us."

"That was before we kissed."

He shook his head. "One kiss can't change everything."

She opened her mouth like she wanted to argue, but she folded her hands in her lap and lowered her gaze. Her shoulders rose as she inhaled, and she lifted her head. "It wasn't just the kiss. My feelings for you have been building for a while now, and I'm realizing how stupid I've been. You're an amazing man, and I'd have to be a fool not to give us a chance."

A pleasant ache spread through his chest at her words, reaching up to his throat. If she meant what she said, his every dream would come true.

"Who else would come rushing to save me from a bad dream in the middle of the night? You've done so much for me. Let me do something for you."

And that was why he couldn't do anything with her right now. She was reeling from a nightmare, and he had been her savior. It was possible she only felt this way because of the situation. He squared his shoulders and looked her in the eyes. "If you still feel this way in the morning, let me know."

"You..." She huffed, and then a small smile curved her lips. "You never stop amazing me. I... You're absolutely right. When I rock your world, I don't want you thinking it's from hero worship."

He chuckled. "I should go. Will you be okay alone? You can come to my apartment if you want. I'll crash on the couch."

"I'm a big girl. I'll be fine."

He rose to his feet, and she grabbed his hand. "Thank you. For everything."

"Any time." He slid from her grasp, afraid if he held on much longer, he'd change his mind and stay. As he turned to leave, the door slammed shut with a *thwack*, making him jump.

Trish gasped. "Was that…?"

He immediately went into ghost hunting mode, and step number one in a haunting was to try and debunk what happened. "Do you have a window open? It could have been a draft." He strode to the window and found it closed tight. Pushing aside the curtain, he felt along the ledge. No air seeped in from outside. The French doors leading to the gallery were shut as well.

"It's ninety-five degrees outside and more humid than Satan's butt crack. The only draft would be from the AC, but I didn't hear it kick on."

"Neither did I." He lifted his hand toward the ceiling vent, but he didn't feel a breeze. After twisting the knob, he tugged on the door, and it opened with ease. He inspected the hinges, closing the door halfway and giving it a slight push to see if gravity might grab onto it and give it the momentum needed to slam with such force. Everything was level. He couldn't debunk it.

"Looks like the ghosts are communicating again." He turned to Trish to gauge her reaction.

She sat on the edge of the bed, looking thoughtful rather than afraid. "I don't think they want you to leave."

"Apparently not." He grinned. "First, they're scaring the crap out of you, and now they're helping you get me into bed?"

She rolled her eyes and returned the smile. "Seriously, though. What if getting married wasn't enough to stop the curse?"

"Natasha said all we had to do was make you a Landry. She didn't say anything about sleeping together." Though he would gladly comply if that was what it would take.

Trish pursed her lips. "I didn't change my name."

He shrugged. "No one changes their name on their wedding day. You have to go to the Social Security office. There are a lot of steps."

"We're not living like we're married either." She rose and paced in front of the bed. "In our vows, we promised to 'live together in matrimony,' but you went home to your apartment. That's not how a marriage works."

"What do you suggest?"

She stopped pacing and put her hands on her hips. "Maybe you need to live here in the house."

He narrowed his eyes. "Are you sure you're not using this as an excuse to get me back into bed?"

She arched a brow. "If I wanted you in my bed, you'd be there. Trust me; you wouldn't be able to resist my wiles."

He couldn't argue with that. It had taken every ounce of willpower he could muster to stop himself from taking her a moment ago. If she tried again, he definitely wouldn't be able to resist. "The bedroom next door is done, right? I could move in there for a while and see if that stops the nightmares."

"Would that make you happy?" she asked into the room. "A husband and wife live under the same roof. Is that what we need to do to stop the curse?"

Silence was the only response.

She looked at him. "I wouldn't mind you staying in the house."

That was all she needed to say. "It's worth a shot."

"I haven't made up that bed yet. Let me get some sheets." She padded down the hall to a closet and pulled out a set of linens.

"I can do that." He took the stack of fabric from her hands, and she returned to the closet to get two pillows.

They made the bed together, and when they finished, she rested her hand on his cheek before leaning in and kissing the other. She didn't pull away. Neither did he. Her nose brushed his beard as she turned her head, and his breathing stilled. Then, she kissed his lips softly before stepping back. "See you in the morning."

"I'm right here if you need me." He always would be.

"I know."

CHAPTER SIXTEEN

*T*rish slept like the dead the rest of the night. She probably would have slept half the day if not for the pesky ray of sunlight slashing across her room and shining in her eyes. Thank goodness it was Saturday. She'd have missed the contractor's arrival if it were a weekday.

Sitting up in bed, she stretched her arms over her head and stilled, listening for sounds of Eric moving around. The house was eerily quiet. Okay, maybe eerie wasn't a fair description. She'd grown used to the sounds of construction. The men made so much noise knocking things around; she wouldn't have noticed if the ghosts were busy.

The silence now unnerved her. Had Eric already left? Did he even spend the night? Her heart sank at the thought of him waiting just until she fell asleep before tiptoeing out and returning to his apartment. Her dad used to do that when she was young. Her anxiety would get so bad she wouldn't be able to sleep without someone in the room. He would promise he'd stay, but it never failed. Every morning when she woke up, he was gone.

"Whoa." She dragged her hands down her face. "Do I

have daddy issues? No, I have anxiety issues. Get a grip, Trish."

Anyway, Eric was not her father. So what if he went back to his apartment? She was a grown woman. She didn't need a babysitter. She swung her legs over the side of the bed and chewed the inside of her cheek. Eric wouldn't do that, would he?

Honestly, she'd half-expected, half-hoped to hear him rummaging around in the kitchen making breakfast, but after the way she'd come on to him, she shouldn't have. Who did she think she was telling him not to even flirt with her and then trying to get him naked? That wasn't fair for her to do. Thank goodness he'd been level-headed about it and stopped her before things went too far. Last night wasn't the time to switch from hands-off to all hands on deck. He was right to make her sleep on it, and now that she had, she was glad for the extra time to think.

She stood and caught a glimpse of herself in the mirror. Her hair was a matted mess, stuck to the right side of her face and sticking out in all directions on the left. Apparently, she'd sweated during her nightmare. "Yikes." No wonder Eric had been able to resist her advances. She looked like a banshee.

After running a comb through her hair, she brushed her teeth and splashed some water on her face. Aside from the sound of the pipes, the house remained silent. She held her breath as she tiptoed into the hall and toward the room Eric slept in. If he wasn't there, she…well, she didn't know how she would feel.

Luckily, it didn't matter. She found him lying on his side, facing the doorway, his head resting on one pillow while he clutched the other to his chest. His lips were slightly parted, and his eyes moved gently beneath his lids.

She stepped into the room and leaned against the wall, watching the rhythmic rise and fall of his chest as he slept. Her stomach fluttered, and a smile curved her lips.

She couldn't fight her feelings for him anymore. He had done so much for her. He was kind, selfless, and hot as sin, and if she were honest, she'd admit he ticked *all* her boxes. Steady job, mature beyond his years, made her laugh…check, check, check. They got along like they'd been friends forever, and the physical attraction was off the charts. The only box she thought he didn't check was the possibility of something long-term.

Yes, he had a reputation of not staying in relationships long, but maybe Sean was right. Maybe he just hadn't found the right woman yet. Maybe *she* could be the right woman. Even if not, the unchecked box in question was the *possibility* of something long-term. How would she know if it were possible unless she gave it a chance?

As she shifted her weight, the floor creaked, and Eric's eyes fluttered open. He sucked in a sharp breath, confusion clouding his features for a moment. Then he smiled. "Good morning, beautiful."

"Hey there, handsome." She returned the smile but didn't move from her spot on the wall.

"What time is it?" His voice was raspy with sleep and sexy as all get-out.

"Ten-thirty."

"Crap. I'm sorry." He sat up and rubbed his eyes.

"What are you sorry for?" She strode to the bed and sat on the edge of the mattress, her stomach tightening from simply being near him.

"For sleeping so late."

"If I remember correctly, you might have been woken by a screaming banshee in the middle of the night."

He laughed. "How is the banshee this morning?"

"No screaming yet. She just woke up too."

"Nightmares?" His gaze wandered over her body before returning to her eyes.

"None. I think you and I being under the same roof did the trick." She scooted closer. "Will you stay here until we're sure the curse is broken?"

"I'll stay as long as you like if it'll keep you from having another episode like last night."

"Speaking of last night. You told me to let you know if I still felt the same." She drummed her fingers on her thighs. "I do."

He searched her eyes. "Are you sure?"

She inhaled deeply, drawing her shoulders toward her ears before letting out her breath. "I am. I had this idea, this plan of how things should be, and I completely ignored the way things *are*. I'm tired of fighting my feelings for you. I've liked you for a long time, and I want to see where it goes. I want to be more than friends if you're still interested."

"You're my wife. Of course I want to be more than friends."

She smiled. "Obviously, we'll still get the annulment so we can do things right. Like the schoolyard rhyme goes: first comes love, *then* comes marriage. We did it backward."

"Well…"

She couldn't let him say the words perched on his tongue. Not yet. So, she did the only thing she could and crushed her mouth to his.

He inhaled quickly through his nose as if the act surprised him, but as she rested her hand on his bare chest, he relaxed into the kiss, cradling the back of her head with his palm. His skin was soft, the muscles beneath firm and defined. Tall and lean, he had the body of a sprinter, and she couldn't wait to explore every inch of it.

Trailing her fingertips down his chest and across his stomach, she memorized the way he felt beneath her touch. His muscles tightened as she neared the waistband of his shorts, but she skipped getting her hands on the prize...for now.

Instead, she rose to her knees on the mattress and straddled his lap. He moaned as she leaned into him, and when she sat up to peel her shirt over her head, his eyes dilated with desire.

He gripped her waist and let his gaze wander over her body. "You're absolutely beautiful."

"I want you, Eric." She guided his hands to her breasts and held them against her. "Make love to me."

A masculine groan vibrated from his chest as he sat up straight, and, with one hand on her back, the other gripping her thigh, he flipped her over and laid her on the bed.

The feel of his bare skin on hers made her breath catch, and she wrapped her arms around him, holding him tightly as they kissed. She spread her legs, allowing his hips to settle between them. An *mmm* resonated from his throat as he trailed his lips across her cheek to her ear, and dear lord, the sounds he made alone were enough to get her off.

"You have no idea how many times I've imagined this." He pressed his hips into her, his dick rubbing against her clit through the fabric and sending an electric jolt through her core.

"I've got a pretty good idea." If it was half as many

times as she had, it was too many to count. "I hope I don't disappoint."

"Never." He thrust his hips again, and she moaned. "Condoms in your nightstand drawer?"

"Next to the vibrator." She tilted her head, giving him better access to her neck.

"You won't be needing that today, *cher*." His breath against her ear gave her goosebumps, and when he rose from the bed, she immediately missed his warmth. "Don't go anywhere."

She closed her eyes and let out a slow breath as he slipped into the hallway. This was it. Three years of anticipation. Thirty-six months of wanting a man she swore she'd never have. A thousand days of denying herself the pleasure of Eric Landry was coming to an end. Her heart pounded against her ribcage, and she breathed deeply to calm the nervous energy roiling in her stomach.

"Have I told you how beautiful you are?" Eric dropped the condoms on the bedside table.

"The whole box? You're ambitious."

"Didn't you know?" He climbed on top of her and kissed her forehead, her cheek, her lips. "Younger men have a lot more stamina. I could keep you here all day."

"We'll have to eat sometime."

He rose onto his knees and flicked his gaze to her pelvis. "Oh, I plan to."

The heat in his words made a warm shiver run up her spine, and as he lowered his head and brushed his lips to her collar bone, all the nervous tension left her body in a flush of cool release.

The tip of his nose glided along her skin as he moved toward her ear. "I love the way you smell," he whispered, and she shivered. "I hope you don't mind if I take my time. You're too exquisite to rush this." He nipped her earlobe, and, heaven have mercy, no words had ever felt so beautifully sinful to her ears.

His kisses along her chest set her soul on fire, and when he reached her breast, flicking out his tongue to bathe her nipple in wet heat, she moaned. He let out a masculine murmur in response and sucked her nipple into his mouth while rolling the other between his fingers until it hardened into a pearl.

He switched sides, giving her other breast as much attention as the first. Then, he pressed a kiss between them before trailing his tongue down to her navel. Her breath hitched as he rose again, and she licked her lips as he tossed his shorts aside.

His dick strained against the fabric of his dark gray underwear, and the small wet spot at his tip made her core tighten with desire. He caressed her with his gaze, and when he tugged off the rest of her clothes, his eyes heating with need, every nerve ending in her body fired on overdrive. Never in her life had she felt so wanted.

She sat up, palming his cock through the fabric before slipping her hand inside and clutching his flesh. He was thick and hard, and her mouth watered to taste him. He closed his eyes, letting out a slow breath as if her touch was the most wonderful sensation he'd ever felt.

He took her face in his hands, kissing her deeply as he laid her back on the bed. She pushed his underwear down his hips, and he tossed them aside before lying next to her, his length pressing into her thigh. He touched her as if she were made of glass, gently gliding his fingers across her skin, caressing every inch of her.

She held her breath as he brushed her hip, and when he circled her clit, she gasped. He moaned at her reaction, kissing his way down her body before settling his shoulders between her legs. His touch grew firmer. He clutched her thigh, pushing it aside and swiping his tongue from slit to clit.

"Ah!" she gasped, and a sound that she could only describe as a growl rumbled from his chest.

He slipped his arms beneath her legs, digging his fingers into her hips in a possessive, hot as hellfire way. Lifting her head, she watched him lick her, the sensations of heat and wetness driving her wild. He raised his gaze to meet hers, and the feral look in his eyes as he slowly ran his tongue up her sweet spot nearly made her come.

With a wicked grin, he slid a finger inside her. She dropped her head back on the pillow and moaned as he twisted his hand, rubbing the most sensitive spot inside her and sucking her clit between his lips. When she spread her legs even wider, he slipped a second finger inside.

Her orgasm tightened in her core, winding up like a spring and releasing in an explosion that made her see stars. It reached all the way to the top of her head and down to her toes. She cried out, twisting her fingers in his hair as he continued his pursuit, and she rode the wave until she couldn't take it anymore.

She tugged him toward her, taking his mouth with hers and kissing him with a passion that could have set them both ablaze. "I need you inside me."

"Yes, ma'am." He rose and put on a condom before settling between her hips, pressing his tip against her. He looked into her eyes, penetrating to her soul as he pushed inside her.

She gasped as he filled her, and his gaze never strayed from hers as he thrust deeper, stilling as he pressed into her. He opened his mouth like he was going to say something, but he closed it, shaking his head and lowering his body to hers.

She held him, exploring his body with her hands as he nuzzled into her neck and began to move. Slowly at first, he pulled out until only his tip remained inside her. Then he slid back in, pressing his hips into her with a long exhale. He repeated the motion three more times before lifting his head, looking at her like he wanted to consume her, and then thrusting hard.

Electricity sparked below her navel and shimmied up to her chest. He increased his rhythm, his hips pumping faster and harder with her moans of pleasure. "Oh, Trish." His voice was deep, filled with need, and her name on his lips sent her over the edge again.

A second orgasm released like a flood, and she clutched his shoulders, holding him tight to her body as she came. The deepest, sexiest moan she'd ever heard emanated from his chest, and he pushed deep inside her, finding his release.

They lay still, their breaths coming in pants. Sweat slicked Eric's back as she ran her hands over his skin. The feel of his body on hers, his arms wrapped around her in a protective cage, his scent, the sounds he made. Everything about him felt right.

When their breathing slowed, he lifted his head and looked at her with passion-drunk eyes and a goofy grin. "I have no words."

"Neither do I." He was better than she ever imagined.

Eric tossed the condom in the trash and lay on his back, tugging Trish to his side. She snuggled against him and basked in the afterglow of the most anticipated sex of her life. Bright sunlight filtered in through the blinds, signaling it must've been close to midday, but she didn't care. She closed her eyes and rested her hand on his chest, concentrating on the gentle rise and fall until she drifted to sleep.

She could have lain there with him all day if not for her growling stomach. The sound woke her, and she lifted her head to find Eric wide awake.

"Hey there, sleepyhead." He kissed her cheek.

"How long was I out?"

"About an hour."

"Mmm." She inhaled deeply and snuggled closer. "You've always had a calming effect on me. I'm so comfortable when I'm with you; I can't help it."

"I was thinking about last night." He stroked her hair from her face and turned to kiss her forehead. "When I found you, you were clawing at the wall and saying, 'Let her out.'"

She propped her head on her hand. "I was?"

He nodded. "It was the disappointments room."

"What do you think it means?"

"I think we need to reopen it."

CHAPTER SEVENTEEN

"Are you sure this is a good idea?" Trish traced a finger along the scratch marks she'd made on the wall while Eric ran a stud finder over the surface to locate the old doorway.

He'd considered going after the wall with a sledgehammer, but Trish had talked him into minimizing the mess. "The curse isn't the only issue with this house. If we're going to have peace here, we need to set the ghosts free. I don't think they mean to cause us any harm."

"I'm not worried so much about the ghosts as I am your grandma. She's fierce, and I do not want to end up on her bad side."

"Don't worry." The stud finder beeped, and he marked the place on the wall. "I'll protect you from her wrath."

"You're good at protecting."

He stopped and turned to her. "Not that you need it. I know you can take care of yourself."

She shrugged. "It's nice to know someone has my back."

"Always." He held his arm out to her, and she stepped

into his embrace as if she belonged there. She fit perfectly in his arms; they fit perfectly together. "Let's put an end to all the suffering the curse has caused."

She hugged him tightly around the waist, pressing her forehead to his shoulder, and the scent of her hair was almost intoxicating. They'd spent what was left of the morning in bed, not bothering to get up until their stomachs' protesting grew louder than an ornery alligator. Then, Trish had insisted on making him lunch...her "famous" grilled cheese sandwich, which was actually better than he expected. Who knew mayonnaise would be a good substitute for butter on the outside of the bread?

He'd returned to his apartment to pack a bag, and then he'd joined her in the shower. He smiled at the memory. Hopefully, plenty more of those memories would be made, but who knew? All he could do was hope her feelings for him now didn't stem from her fear of the curse. Once Natasha came out and told them they were in the clear, he had no idea how Trish would react.

The annulment made sense. If he was going to spend forever with Trish, he wanted to do it the right way. The wedding itself didn't matter to him, but the reason behind it meant everything.

"Eric?" she said against his shoulder.

"Hmm?"

"You're suffocating me."

"Sorry." He released her, and she rested her hands on his chest.

"I like being in your arms too."

"That's good to know." Because he sure as hell couldn't sense her emotions psychically. He was relying solely on body language and instinct with Trish, and it scared him to death and excited him at the same time. Aside from curses, ghosts, and a fake marriage, this was the most normal relationship he'd ever had.

She turned and placed her palm against the wall. "Let's open this baby up."

"We never should have closed it, to begin with." He poked a hole in the drywall and used a saw to cut out the shape of the former door. Dust rained to the floor and floated in the air as he yanked the wall down.

Trish stepped back, her shoulder lifting right before she rubbed her neck. She shook off the nervous tick and slipped her hand into his. "It feels heavy…the energy. Does that make sense?"

"Wait 'til you step inside. Are you sure you want to go in?"

She eyed the passage. "I have to."

He tightened his grip on her hand and crossed the threshold. She hesitated, hovering just outside the door, her palm slicking with sweat before she followed him through.

"It's just like my dreams," she whispered.

He wrapped an arm around her shoulders. "Remember that I showed you pictures of the space before you moved in. That could have played a role in your nightmares."

She shook her head and stepped from his embrace. "No. I didn't have madness-inducing night terrors because of a few pictures. I was experiencing someone's memories." She gasped and jerked her head to the left and then to the right.

"Are you okay?"

Her shoulder ticked again, and she visibly shuddered. "I thought I saw something, but that's crazy, right?"

"It's not crazy. This room is creepy as hell." He moved

toward the bed and ran his hand over one of the shackles. "Whoever is trapped here, you don't have to stay," he said into the room. "We know your story, and we'll make sure you're remembered so you can rest in peace."

His left arm grew cold as if a spirit were trying to manifest, and goosebumps pricked his skin. "If that's you, I can feel you." He pulled a digital recorder from his pocket and switched it on. "If you speak into this device, I might be able to hear you. Is there anything you want us to know?"

The cold dissipated, and when he looked at Trish, her breath came out in a fog. She gasped, her spine turning rigid, her hands curling into fists as her eyes glazed. Shaking her head frantically, she pressed the heels of her hands to her temples and then against her eyes. She jerked, her spine going rigid again before her posture slumped. "Oh, god."

"What is it?" He touched her arm, but she yanked away and paced to the far wall.

"It's here." She placed her palms flat against the surface. "She was locked in here for days. Weeks until she…"

"Who?" He shined his phone's flashlight on the wall.

"I don't know." She kneeled, running her hands along a seam until she found a hidden latch. Pointing to it, she rose and stepped back. "I'm afraid to open it."

His stomach sank. "I kinda am too. Any guess as to what's in there?"

She looked at him, a sadness filling her eyes so palpable he didn't need his sixth sense to know exactly what she thought was inside. He sucked in a breath, steeling himself, and popped the latch. The door creaked open as if it were a damn horror movie, and Trish clutched his arm. Her nails dug into his skin as he lifted the flashlight and shined it into the small space.

"Holy crap." Trish covered her mouth, and Eric cringed.

The closet couldn't have been more than three feet wide by two feet deep, and the body inside—or rather, the pile of bones—lay tangled in a mass of bloodstained fabric that had browned with age. The wood surrounding the poor woman had been gnawed by hungry insects, probably after they finished with her body, and the scratch marks on the inside of the door said she was placed inside while she was still alive.

"He left her there to die because he couldn't handle her hysterics. She was cursed." Her body trembled, her shaky breaths growing shorter, shallower until she began to hyperventilate. "No. No, I need out. It's…" She raked in a breath and darted toward the door. "I need some air."

Eric followed her out of the room, down the hall, and into her bedroom. She paced to the French doors leading to the gallery and threw them open. By the time he caught up, he found her leaning over the railing, staring at the garden below.

"Trish?"

She gasped and righted herself before spinning toward him. Her eyes were wild, her posture, her behavior…hell, everything about her was different. She didn't look like herself at all. This was nothing like the anxiety attack she'd experienced before their wedding.

"*Cher*, are you okay?" He took her shoulders in his hands, and she shook her head, seeming to snap out of whatever trance had ahold of her.

"That poor woman. She was being driven to madness, and her husband couldn't be bothered to help her." Her posture relaxed, and he wrapped an arm around her, guiding her back inside.

He sank onto the mattress with her. "Is this the same person who's been visiting your dreams?"

She stared straight ahead and nodded. "She showed me what it was like being locked in that tiny space."

"In the room just now?"

"Yes," she whispered.

"How?"

She covered her face with her hands, her expression pinching before she spoke, "She was inside me, I think. I saw through her eyes. The dreams were different. This felt so much more real."

"I can't imagine."

"You don't want to. Trust me." She shivered and folded her arms, hugging herself.

He played the recording he'd made in the room, but no disembodied voices answered them. "We need to get the team out here. Whoever she is, she's trying to make contact, and you and I don't have the skill set required to communicate with her."

"We need to call the police. Her murderer could still be alive, and who knows how many other women could be buried within these walls?"

He shuddered at the thought. "You're right. We do, but let's at least get Blake out here to read the nightgown. He's our best bet at finding out who she is."

He dialed Blake's number. "Hey, man. Remember the disappointments room?"

"Hard to forget a place like that."

"Trish and I opened it again, and...we found a body in the wall."

"Bones," Trish rasped. "It was just bones."

Eric rubbed her back. "A pile of bones in a nightgown. We're about to call the police, and I was hoping you could come out and see what you pick up before they get here."

"I'm on my way."

"Thanks. See you soon."

He pressed End and then looked up the non-emergency number for the New Orleans Police Department. When they answered, he explained the situation.

"What did they say?" Trish asked as he hung up.

"They're sending a canine unit with a cadaver dog."

"I saw a movie once where a couple rented out their rooms through one of those travel apps. After guests checked in, they drugged them and buried them in the walls and floorboards. It was so disturbing. I can't…" She rubbed her forehead and sucked in a trembling breath.

"Come here. It's going to be okay." He pulled her to his chest and held her tightly.

After a moment, the tension in her muscles eased, and her breathing slowed. With a deep inhale, she pulled from his embrace, straightening. "Thank you. I'm okay now."

"Were you having an anxiety attack earlier?"

"Sort of, I guess. It felt different, but you always have a way of calming me down." She smiled softly. "You're good for me."

His heart swelled at her words. "You're good for me too."

Half an hour passed before Blake arrived. Trish stayed upstairs while Eric answered the door, and he took Blake straight to the room. The police would be there any minute. In hindsight, he should have waited to call them. The woman had been dead for decades. She wasn't going anywhere, but he'd gone into problem-solving mode, as usual.

"I can't believe I didn't pick up on this when I was here before." Blake stood in front of the body.

"I don't think you touched this wall."

"I couldn't have. I'd have felt something if I did."

"Hi, Blake." Trish entered the room, and Eric held out his arm. She went to his side, stepping into his embrace, and Blake cut his gaze between them, his brow raising in question. "You'll be happy to know Eric and I finally gave in and did the deed."

"She gave in. I've always been willing."

Blake chuckled. "It's about time." He turned and kneeled in front of the bones.

"Do you think you can figure out who she was?" Trish asked.

"I'll try my best." He cracked his knuckles and shook his hands.

"I don't want to hear the horrid details. Her spirit already showed me enough of what happened." She tightened her arms around Eric's waist.

"Her spirit?" Blake turned his head to look at Trish.

"Apparently, being in this house has made Trish sensitive," Eric said.

"She mostly comes to me in dreams, but when we opened the room earlier, it felt like she was inside me. I was really cold, and then I suddenly knew where her body was."

"Interesting," Blake said. "All right, give me a few minutes to see what I can pick up."

Trish rested her hand on Eric's chest as they waited, and he placed his hand over hers, holding it close to his heart. She seemed calm. Her body didn't tremble, and her breathing was slow and relaxed. No sign of anxiety or the curse, though it was hard to tell which was affecting her at any given time.

"Damn." Blake rose to his feet and wiped his hands on his pants. "You weren't kidding about the details being horrid."

"Did you get a name?" Trish asked.

"Not hers, but I heard her screaming at an Albert."

"What did she say?" Eric asked.

Blake cut his gaze to Trish and cringed. "'Why are you doing this? It's not me; this house is cursed.'"

"That's what she showed me," Trish said. "Even in death, she's not free from the damn curse."

"He used the space in the wall to punish her," Blake said. "When she'd get too hysterical, he'd lock her in until she calmed down."

Trish scoffed. "Until one day he'd had enough, and he locked her in for good."

"I can't imagine the smell…" Blake shuddered.

"He was mentally ill," Trish said. "He'd have to be a psychopath to lack empathy like that."

"What about a time frame?" Eric asked.

"Based on their clothing, I'd say late 1800s, but it's hard to tell."

The chime of the doorbell filled the house with music, and Trish pulled from his embrace. "That'll be the police. I'll let them in." She strode out of the room.

Blake waited until her footsteps descended the stairs before he spoke, "How did you and Trish happen?"

"I'm still not sure. We kissed at the courthouse because the judge told us to, and things started happening after that. I guess she got tired of fighting it."

He nodded appreciatively. "Nice."

"Yeah, but this house…" He blew out a puff of air

and glanced at the doorway. "This house has done things to her. I can't tell what's her normal anxiety and what might be the curse affecting her. I don't know how to help her."

"Be there for her." He said it as a matter of fact, like it was the simplest solution in the world.

"If only it were that easy."

"You're doing your best to help the ghosts and break the curse. There's not much else you can do but be there."

"Yeah. You're right." But that was easier said than done. Eric was a problem solver, and it pained him to see Trish hurting. There had to be something more he could do.

"This is where we found the bones." Trish's voice drifted into the room before she led the officers and the dog into the space. The German Shepherd darted straight to the open wall and lay at the threshold.

"That's how he signals a hit," a woman with black hair and dark eyes said. "I'll need you to stay downstairs while we search the premises."

Eric filed out of the room with Blake and Trish, and they settled in the parlor to wait. "I really hope they don't find anyone else," Trish said.

"Me too." Eric took her hand, lacing their fingers together.

"I'll have to question my ability if they do." Blake rested his elbow on the arm of the chair. "I still can't believe I missed that.

"That room was a lot to take in," Eric said. "I'm surprised you don't need therapy after seeing what went on in there."

An hour passed as the police took the dog through every square foot of the main house. Then they checked the grounds, the garage, and Eric's apartment above it. Thankfully, they didn't find any other bodies.

A man with short blond hair descended the steps, carrying a black bag that must've contained the bones. The woman put the dog in the car and met them in the parlor. "Until we can date the remains, this house is considered a crime scene. You'll need to vacate the premises."

"Understood," Eric said, and he looked at Trish. "We can stay at the B and B if you're okay with that."

"Works for me." Trish addressed the officer, "How long do you think it will take?"

"The lab is backed up, so it could be weeks."

"Weeks?" Trish's posture deflated.

"I'll talk to my grandma," Eric said. "I'm sure she can pull some strings and get it done faster. In the meantime, Blake gave us a name. We've got research to do."

CHAPTER EIGHTEEN

*T*wo days. Thanks to Mrs. Landry's money and political pull, it took two days for the lab to date the remains to the 1890s, just like Blake said. Trish knew it would be faster than the weeks the officer suggested, but damn. Must be nice to come from old money in a city like this.

She stayed two nights with Eric—in his old bedroom —at his grandma's B and B. It had felt weird as all get-out sleeping in his bed, fooling around beneath the sheets with his grandma in the house. But Trish was technically married to the man, so she got over that quickly. Besides, Mrs. Landry became giddy as a schoolgirl when she caught them holding hands on the sofa, and her bedroom was clear on the other side of the house.

Who knew? Maybe after all this was over, their relationship could lead to a real marriage. If her feelings for Eric kept growing at their current rate, it wouldn't take long for her to say yes and mean it.

Now, with the crime scene cleared, they moved back into their home, and the whole crew was on their way over for an investigation. With all their abilities combined, they *had* to find a way to help the poor spirits trapped there find peace.

Jason arrived first, and he and Eric went upstairs to set up the equipment. They would measure electromagnetic fields and temperature fluctuations and all that jazz. Trish understood that was part of their routine, but Sean and Emily would be the main attractions at this show. They could see and hear the spirits without getting jumped like what happened to Trish right before they found the bones.

She could have lived without that arctic blast clawing through her body and stealing her breath. It would've been a hell of a lot easier if the spirit had just woken her up the first night and said, "My bones are in the wall. Will you please get them out?"

But, hey. She got her point across, and that was what counted. "Message received," Trish mumbled as she strode across the foyer to answer the door.

Emily and Sean stood on the porch, and Blake pulled into the driveway as Trish invited them in. Sean carried a duffle bag on his shoulder. "I've got the rest of the equipment," he said.

"Eric and Jason are upstairs. Third door on the left." She took Emily's purse and carried it to a table in the parlor.

"Knock, knock," Sydney called from the porch.

"Come on in." Trish met them at the door and locked it behind them. "The guys are already upstairs."

"I can take a hint." Blake kissed Sydney's cheek and headed up to the room.

When he was out of sight, Emily crossed her arms. "You cannot tell us, via text, you and Eric are a couple and then not call to elaborate."

"Sorry." Trish rested a hand on her hip. "We were a little busy with the dead woman in the wall. I've been with him every waking…and sleeping…moment since."

Emily smiled. "It's about time."

She laughed. "That's what Blake said."

"And he's right," Sydney said. "What took you so long?"

"Oh, like neither of you hesitated or made any bad decisions in your relationships. Cut me some slack."

"All right. We better get up there before they start without us." Emily led the way to the stairs. "What about the curse? When's Natasha getting back in town?"

"Day after tomorrow. When the ghost jumped me, I had a moment where I panicked, but it's fuzzy in my mind. Other than that, I haven't had a nightmare or a hint of paranoia since Eric and I… Since we started acting like a couple."

"Magic sex saved the day," Sydney laughed.

Trish snorted. "I think the actual marriage part helped too. Of course, Natasha said the curse would give me periods of reprieve where I'd feel normal, so who knows? Maybe this is the calm before the storm." She paused at the second-floor landing. "You haven't had any visions of Eric and me, have you? Any hints on how it might turn out?"

"I've got a handle on my gift now. I don't have many visions unless I want to. Would you like me to try?"

She bit her lip. "No. Being with him feels good. I don't want to lose it too soon, and knowing if he's going to dump me would ruin what we have."

Sydney nodded. "Good decision."

"Here we go." Trish motioned toward the bedroom, and they paced across the floor to join the guys in the disappointments room. Eric caught her gaze as they stepped through the door, and his smile warmed her to her core.

They'd set up their equipment on a table in the center of the room. Trish recognized a small black rectangle—a digital recorder for capturing voices—and a gray device with stoplight-colored LEDs—a contraption that would illuminate if it sensed an electromagnetic field. Supposedly, ghosts could manipulate energy. She'd leave the technical stuff up to the team.

Trish walked to Eric's side and slipped her hand into his. "We think we know who the woman in the wall might be."

"We researched the property records," Eric said, "and we found an Albert who owned the house in the 1890s."

"He married Imogene in 1889," Trish said. "She was listed on the census with him in 1890, and that was the last record of her existence. He didn't include her in his household in 1900. No death record. She just disappeared."

Sydney shook her head. "He erased her from his life."

"From existence," Emily said. "I'm glad you found her name. It'll help us if we have to summon her."

Sean stiffened. "Let's hope it doesn't come to that. Summoning spirits is dangerous business. You never know what else might come through."

"We'll be careful," Trish said. "We have to help her."

"Let's get started." Emily lit a tall, white candle and placed it in the center of the table before dimming the lamp next to Jason's feet. "Imogene? If you or anyone else is here, we would love to talk to you."

"The objects on the table can help you communicate,"

Sydney said. "They can hear you if we can't, or you can make the lights turn on or the candle flame flicker."

Trish held her breath, waiting for something to happen. The floor creaked, and she started, sucking in a sharp breath and tightening her grip on Eric's hand.

"That was me," Jason said. There's a loose board here.

She let out her breath. "See? This is why I don't do investigations with y'all. I'm not afraid of ghosts, but I'm a bundle of nerves anyway."

"You get used to it." Eric tugged from her grasp and rested his hand on the small of her back in the way that always eased her tension. "Try talking to her."

She wiped her sweaty palms on her pants and cleared her throat. "Imogene? Do you remember me? You've shown me some things, awful things that happened to you." She looked at Emily, who shook her head, and then at Sean.

"I'm not sensing anything but residual energy," he said.

"Natasha didn't clear this room." Trish paced to the secret door in the wall and peered inside. Sadness weighed heavy in her heart.

"We had already sealed it before she got here." Eric let out a hard sigh. "I never should have allowed that to happen."

Trish returned to his side. "It's your grandma's house. You were respecting her wishes."

"If anyone is with us, will you please move close to the table?" Jason said. "Touch the devices on it or speak into them."

"What your husband did to you was horrible," Emily said. "If you'd like to talk about it, we're here to listen."

They waited in silence for a few seconds before Sydney picked up the recorder. "Let's play this back."

A sickening sensation formed in Trish's stomach as they listened. Their voices came through clearly, but only silence answered them.

"Maybe she already moved on since you found her body," Jason said.

"No." Trish glanced at the closet. "Don't ask me how I know, but she's still here." She could sense it somehow, feel it in her soul as if she had a connection with the spirit. It made no sense, but she knew it was true.

"She's right," Eric said. "I can feel her despair. The room has a lingering sadness, but her emotions are like a current running through it. She's here."

"We're going to have to summon her." Emily moved toward the table and gestured for the others to join her.

"Can you cross her over?" Trish asked. The poor woman needed peace.

"We can talk to her, let her know it's okay for her to leave, but we can't force her to the other side." Emily took her hand and reached for Sean.

"You need to be trained in witchcraft or Voodoo to have that ability," Sean said as he reached for Blake's hand. "We'll do what we can."

They all joined hands in a circle around the table. Trish's palms were cold and clammy, but Eric's and Emily's were dry and warm. How did they do stuff like this all the time without losing it? Her heart pounded so hard and fast it felt like it would bust through her ribcage any second.

A whisper sounded in her right ear, and she tensed as it seemed to pass through her head and come out on the left side like listening to something in stereo through headphones. She should have taken an Ativan before they started this. Heaven knew she needed to calm the eff down.

"Are you okay?" Eric squeezed her hand.

"Yeah," she lied.

"You can wait downstairs if you need to," Emily said. "If she's here, we'll call her out."

"No, I need to stay. She knows me." If Trish were a ghost and a bunch of strangers were trying to force her to talk, she'd make herself scarce too. She'd rather Imogene feel comfortable speaking with them. The poor woman endured enough torture in life.

"Everyone, take a deep breath to clear your energy," Emily said.

Trish did as she was told, and it did help calm her a little. But she'd need twenty more deep breaths to chase away the adrenaline making her on edge.

"We call on the spirit of Imogene Thompson." Emily's voice was calm and direct. "Come forward and make yourself known."

"Any entities will ill intent are banished from this space," Sean said. "No one may cause us harm."

Trish stared at the candle flame. Was it flickering, or was that her imagination too? She glanced at the others, but no one reacted. "Imogene? Are you here?"

It flickered again, and a chill ran down her spine. "She's here. Do you see her?"

"Where?" Emily asked.

Trish squeezed her eyes shut as goosebumps pricked on her skin. The energy in the room buzzed, thickening around her. "Everywhere."

An arctic blast shot through her chest, cascading down her body and filling her with frigid electricity. *Oh, hell.*

This felt just like when… She gasped as Imogene took hold.

"Trish?" Eric's voice was a distant echo.

The spirit showed Trish her life. The marriage had been arranged, loveless. The curse acted slowly, first making her paranoid, giving her nightmares, making her see and hear things before finally driving her to hysteria.

"I know." Trish's voice was raspy, her throat dry. "I've been going through it too, but you're free now. You can move on. It's over."

"She's communicating with you?" Sydney asked, and Trish nodded.

"Please, I don't need to see the torture again. He can't hurt you anymore." Her breath hitched. Her muscles tensed, and a sharp pain shot through her skull. She tried to swallow the sandpaper from her throat, but she couldn't make herself move.

"It's not over." The words coming from her mouth were not her own. "I tried to warn you."

"Oh my god, Sean." Emily grasped Trish's shoulders. "The spirit jumped her."

No kidding, she wanted to say, but she'd lost control. "I need to lie down," came out instead.

Imogene made her walk to the bed, and she lay on the dusty surface. "This house is cursed."

Eric kneeled by her side and took her hand. She could feel his touch, hear his voice, but she couldn't make herself respond. "What else do we need to do, Imogene?" he asked. "I'm a Landry, and Trish is my wife. You're free to leave."

"Not free," she rasped. "Let me up! Let me up!" She shot off the bed and cowered in the corner, wrapping her arms around herself.

"Shit." Eric rushed toward her. "How do we get the spirit out of her?"

"Imogene," Emily said. "The man who hurt you is gone. We found your body, and no one can hurt you again. You need to let Trish go. It's over."

"It's not over." Her throat felt like she'd swallowed razor blades, her head like her skull was splitting.

"Trish, you need to take control." Emily clutched her arm. "Tell her to leave your body. You are the lady of this house, so she has to obey you. Focus."

Trish gathered her strength and focused it on the pain in her head. *You've shown me enough. I'm trying to help you, but you can't keep jumping me. Let me go.*

If she had control of her body, she'd have squeezed her eyes shut and clenched her fists, but she still couldn't make herself move. *Imogene, you're holding me prisoner like Albert did to you. Please let me go.*

Electricity jolted through her body, making her spine rigid before she collapsed into Eric's arms.

"Trish?" He held her to his chest. "*Cher*, talk to me."

"Holy fuck." Her words, not Imogene's. *Hallelujah.*

"Thank goodness." Eric kissed the side of her head. "Let's get you to your room so you can lie down."

"No." She pulled from his embrace, a sudden spike of anger burning in her chest that didn't feel like her own. "I'm fine." She whirled toward Sean and Emily. "What the hell, guys? You told me ghosts can't do that unless they're invited in. I never gave her permission to use my body." The words flew from her mouth laced with enough venom to take down an elephant, but she couldn't stop herself.

Emily flinched, and Sean wrapped an arm around her protectively. "They normally can't," she said.

"I don't think you're okay," Eric said, his expression wary.

She looked at her friends, and they all appeared shocked and concerned, their eyes wide, brows raised. "What are you staring at?" She flung her arms in the air. "Y'all make this ghost hunting business out to be completely safe and fun. You lied to me. It's neither."

"Trish, sweetheart." Eric took her shoulders in his hands.

Her body shuddered, the spike of adrenaline raking through her veins like razor blades, tearing her up from the inside out. The words were hers, weren't they? No one had made her lash out...or had they? *God! I don't know what's happening.* "Don't you dare tell me to calm down."

"I'm not. I just want you to take a breath with me, okay?" He cupped her face in his hands and moved closer. "In through the nose, out through the mouth. Come on." He inhaled deeply, and she followed his lead.

As she breathed, he inched closer, resting his forehead against hers. They inhaled again, taking four more breaths together before the rage inside her simmered. After two more breaths, it snuffed out, leaving her raw and empty.

"Oh, god." She looked at her best friend. "Emily, I'm sorry. I don't know what came over me."

"Was it you?" Blake asked.

She nodded. "I think so. I got so mad all of a sudden. I'm sorry for lashing out." Holy crap, that was way out of character. She scanned her memory, trying to recall a time she'd felt that much anger. Never toward her friends.

"Let's get out of this room." Eric wrapped an arm around her, and they all went downstairs to sit in the parlor.

Trish clutched his hand and leaned into his side on the

sofa. Her ears burned with embarrassment. "I have an appointment to get my meds adjusted next week. Between trying to start a business and the curse, the stress has messed me up. I'll be better soon."

"It's okay." Emily gave her a sympathetic smile. "What you've gone through would take a toll on anyone. You're lucky you've got Eric to take care of you."

"Tell me about it." She laughed, though she wasn't sure why. Nothing about this was funny. "Seriously, though. How was she able to do that to me?"

Emily looked at Sean, and something unsettling passed between them.

"My best guess is the curse forged a connection between you and Imogene," Sean said. "It stripped away whatever natural protections you had in place and made you vulnerable to spirits."

"Oh, man." She sank in her seat. "You said spirits plural. Does this mean I'm like you now? Will others…?"

"It's possible," Emily said. "Either way, it won't hurt for you to learn some psychic protection."

"If I ignore it long enough, it'll go away, right? It worked for you for years."

Emily glanced at Sean before looking at her. "I wouldn't recommend that."

"I can teach you how to protect yourself." Eric wrapped an arm around her. "I have to keep my shields up all the time, or I'll go crazy."

"We can all help you," Sydney said.

The knot in her chest loosened. She was so damn lucky to have these friends. "Thanks. In the meantime, I guess I'll still be plagued with nightmares until Imogene decides to move on."

"We need to figure out why she thinks she's stuck

here," Eric said. "Her body isn't in the wall, so there must be something else." He looked at Trish, his brows drawing together. "That bout of anger didn't seem like you in there. I don't think the curse has lifted yet. It must be holding her here."

Trish's phone buzzed in her back pocket, so she tugged it out as Eric continued, "We need to write down everything she said so we can tell Natasha when she comes. Hopefully she can tell us what to do."

"That could be an issue." Trish's shoulders slumped as she stared at the message on the screen. "Her cousin took a turn for the worse and is back in the hospital. She doesn't know when she'll be back."

"Well, crap," Emily said.

Sean leaned forward, resting his elbows on his knees. "Call her."

"She's busy with her cousin." Trish hated to be a burden. It was one thing for her friends to drop everything to help her with this, but she hardly knew Natasha.

"And you're not safe in this house as long the ghost has access to your body." He dialed his phone and laid it on the coffee table.

Natasha answered on the first ring. "Hello, Sean. You must be with Trish and Eric."

"Yes, ma'am, I am, and we could use some advice. You're on speaker."

"I've got a few minutes," she said. "Shoot."

"We got married." Trish leaned toward the phone. "But before we did, I sort of formed a connection with a spirit here. She's been jumping me." She and Eric took turns explaining everything that had happened since their last meeting with the priestess.

"Mm-hmm." Natasha urged them to continue.

"We got her body out of the wall," Trish said, "but she says it's not over and she can't move on."

"Sounds to me like the curse is still alive and kickin'," Natasha replied.

Trish's blood drained from her head to her toes. She knew it was still affecting her, despite trying to blame it all on her anxiety, but she'd hoped against hope the priestess would say otherwise.

It didn't make sense. The lady of the house was a Landry now, so why was the spirit stuck? *Wait.* What if the curse wasn't holding Imogene here? What if it was the other way around? "It can't be broken, can it? Not while a Thompson woman resides in the house."

"Where are her bones now?"

"They're at the coroner's office." Trish tapped a finger against her lips, an idea forming in her mind. Imogene died tragically after the hex...and her husband...tortured her for years. Now her bones were lying in a locker at the morgue. It was no wonder she refused to pass on. "She needs a proper burial, doesn't she?"

"That could do the trick."

"At the very least, it would be the right thing to do. People were uber-religious and superstitious back then. If she knows her bones weren't laid to rest, she might think she has to stay on this plane."

"You're more capable than you thought," Natasha said. "Get her remains into a tomb. I'll call a friend of mine to pay you a visit when you do, and she can clear her out if she still refuses to leave."

"Thank you, Natasha," Eric said.

"I hope your cousin feels better soon," Trish added before Sean hung up and returned his phone to his pocket.

"I can call Rose Thompson, see if she'll agree to put her in the family tomb," Eric said.

Trish shook her head. "We need to see if any of her blood relatives are still around. I doubt she'd want to spend eternity with the man who murdered her."

CHAPTER NINETEEN

Trish walked by Eric's side toward Lafayette Cemetery Number Two. Towering oaks shaded the sidewalk, providing a bit of relief from the torturous summer sun. She moved behind him as they passed through the middle of a tour group gathered outside the gates, and Eric nodded a hello to the guide.

He did that a lot, as if all the tour guides of New Orleans were part of some secret society of camaraderie, even though they were competing for the same tourists. Maybe she would share the same fellowship with other B and B owners one day. She was sure as hell ready to put all this behind her and work on her new life as a business-woman...with Eric by her side. Her lips curved into a smile at the thought.

She had stayed with him in the apartment above the garage the past three nights. Imogene's ghost seemed to be confined to the main house, so as long as Trish didn't set foot inside, she was fine. Well, her anxiety was still doing a number on her, but she saw her doctor yesterday and upped the dose of her meds. Now all she had to do was make it through the lovely side effect that made her want to jump out of her own skin. Honestly, it felt as bad as the curse, but at least she didn't have to solve a mystery to end the effects.

Once they laid Imogene to rest, Trish would be back to normal by the end of the week. *Hopefully.* If this didn't stop it, she'd probably end up in a padded cell.

They entered the cemetery and walked past the rows of above-ground tombs. Some were well-kept with painted exteriors and flowers adorning the vases in front, while others looked ancient and crumbling, the plaster worn away to reveal the brick and mortar beneath.

Eric pointed to a massive white tomb with a stone angel sitting atop it. "That's my family's grave."

"It's beautiful."

"Grandma keeps it well-maintained. Tombs here say as much about family status as houses."

"How many generations are buried there?"

"Too many to count."

She slipped her hand into his. Cemeteries used to creep her out, but the way New Orleanians buried their dead brought her a sense of comfort. When someone died, they placed the body on a shelf near the top of the tomb, which acted like an oven in the Louisiana heat, essentially cremating the remains over the course of a year. When the next person in the family died, they would move what was left of the bones to the bottom to rest with all their relatives, and the newly deceased would get their turn on the shelf.

She spotted an older woman wearing a black dress, her white hair pulled back in a scarf, and they made their way toward her and the minister standing by an open tomb. "I still can't believe we pulled this off."

Eric squeezed her hand. "We solved a mystery and are laying a woman to rest after more than a century. Give us a little credit."

"I'm so glad we were able to find a living relative." Imogene would surely be at peace once her remains were reunited with her sisters'. She approached the woman and offered her hand. "Adelaide? I'm Trish, and this is Eric."

Adelaide shook her hand and then his. "It's nice to meet you both."

"Thank you so much for doing this," Trish said.

"When you told me her story, I knew I had to help. Imogene belongs with her family."

"Yes, she does." Eric rested his hand on Trish's back as the minister gave the *ashes to ashes, dust to dust* speech.

She teared up when he placed the bag of bones into the tomb, and she stepped forward, resting her hand on the smooth stucco. "You endured more pain in life than anyone should experience. May you finally rest in peace."

Two men in work clothes appeared out of nowhere to put the stone cover on the opening and lock it into place. They must've been there the whole time, just out of sight. Stealth was probably part of the job description.

Trish traced her finger over the newest name added to the marble plaque.

Imogene Brown – March 8, 1868 – 1890*

"I'm glad you used her maiden name." Trish flinched, her right shoulder jerking upward as her muscles crawled beneath her skin. She clutched her arms and tried to keep a neutral expression. Digging her fingers into her skin eased the sensation, but the unintelligible whisper moving from her right ear to her left made her shiver.

Luckily, Adelaide either didn't notice or pretended not to. "Since the last record of her alive was the 1890 census, I used that as the date of death. Her situation is explained in the family archives, and the asterisk indicates that."

"Thank you again." Trish shook her hand and walked with Eric out of the cemetery.

"Are you okay?" he asked as they made a right on the sidewalk and headed home. "You've still got that shoulder tick."

"Side effects of my medication. It'll go away eventually."

"Trish…" The look on his face said he wasn't buying it.

She sighed and looked at the clock on her phone. "I'll be fine. We better hurry. Natasha's friend will be there soon."

When they got home, Eric opened the front door, but Trish hesitated to enter. The last thing she needed was for Imogene to jump her the moment she stepped inside, and based on the way her skin crawled at the cemetery, the ghost didn't cross over when they placed her remains in the tomb. Otherwise, the curse would be gone…in theory. "Can you do your thing and see if you feel her?"

"Sure." He stopped in the foyer and closed his eyes. "I don't feel any emotions other than my own. She's not manifesting right now, but it doesn't mean she isn't here."

"Hello, there. Are you Trish?" A woman with curly, dark brown hair and an umber complexion ascended the front steps. She wore a purple silk blouse with black pants, and she smiled as she approached. "I'm Odette, Natasha's friend."

Trish let out a breath of relief and returned the smile. "Perfect timing. Come on in." She motioned for Odette to enter and waited a beat to make sure she didn't recoil from the spirit energy before following her inside and closing the door.

"Natasha tells me you need to sever a bond with a ghost?" She set her bag on a side table and pulled out a jar of yellow powder.

"We just got back from burying her remains with her family. I hoped that would be enough to make her cross over, but after what we've been through, I don't think it was." She stepped to Eric's side, and he slid his arm around her waist.

Odette retrieved a purple candle and a cigarette from her bag before kneeling in the foyer. "You did the right thing by calling me out. She's still here, and she thanks you."

Oh, jeez. Would Trish ever feel normal in the place? "Why hasn't she left? Can you make her leave?" She flicked her gaze around the room as if she could see the spirit. "No offense, Imogene. We both need some peace."

"I'll take care of it. Your house will be ghost-free by the time I'm done." She dipped her hand into the jar and scooped out the contents. "This is cornmeal. I'm going to draw a vévé on your floor with it, but I'll clean it up when I'm done."

"What's that?" Trish asked.

"It's a symbol that represents Baron Samedi, the Voodoo loa of the dead. I'll call on him to open the gates and help the spirit cross over." Resting one hand on the floor, she poured the cornmeal out the side of her fist, creating an intricate design of a cross with a coffin on either side.

"Does he always listen?" Eric asked.

She dusted off her hands. "To me, yes. We have a very

strong connection." She lit the candle and pressed her palms together. "Baron Samedi, please hear my request. I ask you to open the gates to the spirit world and allow Imogene passage to your realm."

The energy in the room thickened, and the hair on the back of Trish's neck stood on end. She rubbed her arms and looked at Eric, who nodded, confirming he felt it too. Thank goodness she wasn't the only one this time, though she doubted Eric had the nausea and tension running through his body like she did. He was always so calm. He'd become her rock through all of this, her grounding force in a hurricane.

Odette opened the cigarette and sprinkled the contents onto the vévé. "I offer tobacco in exchange for your help, and you know the rum is yours anytime you want it." She rose to her feet. "I run a distillery in his honor. Baron Samedi loves his rum."

"Is that it? Is she gone?"

"Not yet. First, we need to sever her connection to you. May I?" She held out her hands palms up.

Trish placed her hands in Odette's and swallowed the sourness creeping up the back of her throat. "Is this going to hurt?"

"You'll just feel a little pinch."

"That's exactly what the nurse tells her patients before she jabs them with a two-inch needle. I worked in an urgent care clinic."

Odette chuckled. "It'll be over before you know it. Close your eyes."

She glanced at Eric, and apprehension drew his brows together. A tendon in his neck protruded like he was clenching his jaw, and she tried to reassure him with a smile before she closed her eyes.

"Oh, she has her hooks in you deep," Odette said. "She gives you nightmares, makes you see things."

"Too many things." She took a deep breath, trying to slow her racing pulse.

"Can you help her?" Eric asked, his voice laced with worry.

"Absolutely. Trish, I want you to look inward and feel the weight in your chest. There's a thickness that feels like it's trying to drag your heart downward. Do you sense it?"

She squeezed her eyes tighter and focused on her chest. Sure enough, a heavy ball, like a shotput, sat just below her left breast. She'd never noticed it before, but it was unmistakable now. "I feel it."

"Good. Now imagine a cord running from you to Imogene's spirit. Can you see the ghost in your mind?"

"I don't know what she looks like. Everything she showed me was through her eyes."

"Imagine a shadow, then. A cord running from the heaviness in your heart to the shadow."

She pictured the outline of a woman, gray mist billowing with long hair and a flowing gown. "Got it."

"This is where that pinch is going to happen. On the count of three, I need you to cut the cord. I'm going to help you do it. Are you ready?"

Every muscle in her body tensed. She wanted to recoil. Odette's hands felt electric, like she was passing energy into her and making her soul vibrate with heat. She forced in another breath, and with her exhale, she said, "I'm ready."

"One…"

Trish tightened her grip on Odette's hands.

"Two…"

She held her breath and focused on the weight.

"Three…" Odette sent a jolt of energy through her hands. It shot up Trish's arms and zapped her chest as she imagined a pair of scissors cutting the cord binding her to the ghost.

Pain flared white-hot through her body. She felt electrocuted. Burned from the inside out. She tried to scream, but she couldn't emit a sound, so she doubled over. Eric caught her before she could hit the ground, and he helped her to a chair.

"I've got you, *cher*. Please tell me it's over now." He held her to his chest and stroked her hair from her face.

"It's done," Odette said. "The moment the bond severed, Baron Samedi took her home."

"Thank you," Trish croaked, and she sat up straight. The heavy weight in her chest had lifted, and the air in the house felt lighter.

"I'd like to smudge the property to be sure there are no more lingering spirits. I can feel Natasha's blessing is still in place, so this will only take a minute. You can wait here."

Trish nodded and leaned her head back on the chair, her throat thickening, tears gathering in her eyes. "It's finally over, Eric. Things can go back to normal now."

"They sure can."

A few minutes later, Odette returned downstairs. "I smudged the extra room up there too. It had some bad residual energy, but it should be cleared now. Your home is free from all spirit energy."

"What about the curse?" Eric asked. "Is that gone too?"

"I deal with the dead. Curses are Natasha's thing." She took a hand-held vacuum from her bag and kneeled in front of her vévé. "Thank you for your assistance, Baron

Samedi. Please close the gates." After swiping her hand through the drawing, she blew out the candle, vacuumed up the mess, and returned the items to her bag.

Trish stood and shook her hand. "Thank you so much. We appreciate you taking the time to help us."

"My pleasure, Trish, Eric. Good luck with your curse."

"Hopefully that did the trick," Trish said.

Odette bowed her head. "Have a nice day."

CHAPTER TWENTY

*E*lation. It was the only way to describe what Eric felt as he looked at Trish. She stood in the kitchen, leaning against the counter, a half-drunk glass of sparkling wine in her hand. Her smile brightened her eyes, and the way she gazed back at him made his stomach tighten.

"I have never felt more relieved, happy, optimistic, and horny in my entire life," she said.

"Horny?" He chuckled and stepped toward her, tucking her hair behind her ear.

She caught her bottom lip between her teeth as her gaze dipped to his mouth. "You have no idea. The way you look out for me, just knowing you're going to be there to catch me if I fall…it's such a turn-on."

He looked into her eyes and cupped her cheek in his hand, running his thumb over her soft, smooth skin. "I will always be there for you, Trish." He pressed a kiss to her lips. "Whenever you need me."

"I need you now."

He took the glass from her hand and set them both on

the counter before sliding his palms down to her butt and tugging her hips to his. "I would love to take care of you." *For the rest of your life.* But he didn't dare say that part out loud. Not yet. Not until he was sure she felt the same.

"Let's take care of each other." She gripped the back of his neck and pulled him in for another kiss.

Her lips felt like velvet against his, and the slightly sweet taste of wine on her tongue made his head spin. Trish was everything he dreamed she would be...better than he ever imagined. If this was truly over, if the curse was lifted like he hoped it was, he needed to talk to her. To find out if she wanted this to be forever like he did.

He broke the kiss to say the words, but he couldn't ignore the hunger in her eyes...primal, urgent. There would be time for talk after he satiated her need...and he planned to satisfy her again and again.

"What?" She slid her hands to his pecs and leaned back.

"You're so beautiful." He tugged her to his chest and took her mouth once more.

She moaned as he kissed her, and when her fingertips found the hem of his shirt, she pulled it upward, over his head. He tossed it aside and removed her top, revealing a lacey blue bra. His favorite one. He couldn't wait to find out if she had on the matching panties, so he unbuttoned her pants and worked them down her hips. *Jackpot.*

She grinned wickedly as she toed off her shoes and kicked her pants aside. Walking her fingers across his shoulder, she moved behind him before pressing her lips to the back of his neck. The gesture made him shiver as she continued placing soft kisses down his spine. When she reached the waistband of his jeans, she flicked out her tongue and licked all the way back up.

"I love the way your skin tastes." She pressed her front to his back and nipped his neck as she slid her hand around to grip his cock through his jeans.

He groaned at the sensation, his eyes fluttering shut for a moment before he inhaled deeply and turned around. The heat in her eyes could have burned him to ash, and he gripped her hips, lifting her onto the counter before spreading her legs and pulling her against him.

The need in her expression was nearly overwhelming, and it lit a fire in his core, fueling his own desire. He removed her bra and cupped her breasts, teasing her nipples with his thumbs as he kissed her. Fingers tangled in his hair, she held him close and ran a hand down his back to grip his butt.

"You know," she said against his lips as she unbuttoned his jeans. "If we were open for business, this would be such a health code violation."

"We better have as much fun as we can before then." His breath came out in a hiss as her fingers wrapped around his cock.

"I plan to." She slid off the counter and dropped to her knees, yanking down his pants along the way. "I love your dick."

"I love…" He sucked in a sharp breath, stopping himself from finishing the sentence the way he wanted to. "I love that you love it."

She flicked out her tongue, licking the sensitive under-side of his tip, and his balls tightened. "God, you taste good." She circled his head before taking him into her mouth, and his knees nearly buckled.

The wetness and heat enveloping him, and Trish's gaze locked on his as she sucked him, were enough to make him come after two strokes. He fisted his hands at his sides, getting himself under control before this ended too soon.

She took him in as far as her mouth would allow and then pulled away, her lips gliding over his flesh before taking him in again. She repeated the decadent motion three more times before releasing him and rising to her feet.

The cool air against his wet cock made it twitch, and she licked her lips as she shimmied out of her panties. With one hand on her back, he pulled her to his body and slid the other hand between her legs. An *mmm* emanated from her lips as his fingers brushed her clit, and she closed her eyes, her head falling back as she enjoyed his touch. God, he loved making her feel good.

She gasped when he slipped two fingers inside her, and she opened her eyes, pinning him with her fiery gaze. She was warm and so damn wet he couldn't hold back anymore. Gripping her hips, he turned her toward the counter. She spread her legs and leaned forward, giving him access to her sweet spot, and he rubbed his tip against her folds.

"Take me, Eric. I need you."

His skin turned to gooseflesh with her words. He pushed inside her, and her breath came out as a long, slow *ahhh*. He stood there pressing into her, reveling in the way she felt wrapped around him, squeezing him, but her need grew with every passing moment. He wouldn't make her wait anymore.

He pulled out halfway, moving his hips in short strokes before plunging deep inside her. She gasped and moaned with every thrust, growing wetter and hotter as he pumped his hips. Leaning forward, he slid his hand to her clit and stroked it as he moved. She gripped the countertop, her knuckles turning white as her climax built.

She cried out with her release, and a tidal wave of ecstasy crashed into him as he came. Both of them panting, their bodies slick with sweat, they stilled. He held her to his chest and kissed her cheek before slipping out and turning her around to face him.

Her eyes glazed, and she leaned into him, wrapping her arms around him. "Holy crap, that was hot."

"No kidding." His legs trembled, so he adjusted his stance.

She lifted her head from his shoulder. "I think we should spend the rest of the evening in bed. I wouldn't mind an encore when you're ready."

He chuckled and glanced at his dick, which was still giving her a standing ovation. "I'm ready when you are."

"Dating a younger man has its benefits." She took his hand and led him upstairs to her bedroom.

They made love three more times before they finally wore themselves out, and Eric couldn't think of a moment in his life when he'd ever been happier. Trish was the one. He had no doubt in his mind that he wanted to spend forever with her, and if tonight was any indication, it was probable she felt the same.

Still, he couldn't bring himself to tell her yet. She lay on her side, her back snuggled against his front. Her breathing deepened, taking on a slow, smooth rhythm as her body relaxed.

Man up and say the words. His fear of rejection had controlled him long enough. It was time Trish knew exactly how he felt.

"I love you," he whispered, but she didn't respond. He'd waited too long, and she'd fallen asleep.

This was a good thing. Saying it like that had been cowardly. The first time she heard him say the words, it needed to be face to face. She needed to know he meant it.

He closed his eyes and fell asleep with the woman he loved in his arms. When he woke, the bed was cold, and he found Trish wearing a pink silk robe, standing at the French doors leading to the gallery. Her back was to him, and as he opened his mouth to tell her good morning, a wave of dread washed over him.

Something about her posture was off. She was stiff, her stance narrow, and as he cleared his throat, sitting up in the bed, her shoulder hitched the way it always did when the curse had ahold of her.

He closed his eyes as he let out a slow breath. They'd done everything right, exactly as Natasha had instructed them. Their marriage was legal. They'd laid the ghost to rest. Why the fuck was this not over?

Trish meant the world to him. She *was* his world, and seeing her like this, watching her struggle with a pain his ancestors caused a century ago tore him to shreds.

He tossed the sheets aside. "Trish?"

She whirled around, her eyes tight with worry. "They're here." Her voice was raspy.

"Who's here?" He scooted to the edge of the bed and rested his feet on the floor.

"They whisper." She clamped her hands over her ears. "They're inside my head."

He slowly rose, taking care not to startle her. "No one's inside you, *cher*. It's the curse trying to mess with your mind. You've got to fight it."

"Fight it?" She tilted her head at an odd angle. "It's part of me. They're part of me."

"Who is?" He opened his senses, searching the room

for signs of another spirit, for some shred of emotion that could be affecting her, but all he felt was his own pulse pounding in his ears. No one was there.

"The whispers." Her bottom lip quivered.

"What are they saying?"

She shook her head, her gaze darting about the room. "I don't know. No! I won't live like this."

"That's right, *cher*. You don't have to accept it. You've got to fight it. I'm here to help you."

Her gaze grew wild, and her hands trembled. "You're part of it. Part of the cause."

"No. No, I'm here to help." He moved toward her, and as she took a step back, he clenched his jaw. He *was* part of it. Hell, he was the reason for all of this. If he hadn't invited Trish into the house, none of this would have happened, and he would never forgive himself for it. "I'm sorry."

"No!" Her shoulder hitched again, and he rushed to her. He took her arms in his hands, but she yanked from his grasp.

"Don't touch me." Her breathing grew shallow, coming in short pants. "Don't ever touch me again!" Her voice grew louder with each word until she screamed. "It's... No!" She clutched her head, her shoulder jerking yet again.

"I can't do this. Ahh!" She dragged her hands down her face as she screamed. Her body quaked, and she clawed at her neck as if she couldn't breathe.

"Trish."

"I won't let you do this!" She shook her head frantically and stomped toward the gallery.

"What are you doing?"

She whirled to face him, and the terror in her eyes

paralyzed him. All the women in the house had succumbed to madness. Now, thanks to him, it was happening to Trish.

"I need some air," she said before turning around and throwing open the gallery doors.

Eric raced toward her, but he tripped on the rug. He hit the floor with a thud, and sharp pain shot from his shoulder to the middle of his back. He scrambled to his feet and darted onto the gallery, but Trish already lay in the garden below.

CHAPTER TWENTY-ONE

*E*ric believed in science. Spirits were forms of energy, and psychic abilities were simply a branch of the discipline that wasn't yet understood. Even Voodoo magic—curses included—was a way of manipulating energy that couldn't be explained. One day, perhaps, it would all make sense, but for now, he took comfort in knowing he wasn't alone. That his friends held the same beliefs, and they looked at paranormal phenomena in the most logical way possible.

But what happened to Trish was nothing short of a miracle.

Two weeks ago, she'd planted a row of hedges beneath the gallery outside her room, and when she went over the edge, they'd broken her fall. She was conscious when he made it outside, and the ambulance arrived five minutes after he called. Scratches, cuts, and bruises covered her body, and the sharp edges of the bushes had torn her robe, but nothing appeared to be broken. She was even lucid enough to ask him to bring her purse and some clothes to the hospital.

He'd done as she requested, texting Natasha and his grandma along the way, and now he sat in the waiting room while the doctor attended to Trish.

This was his fault. He recognized the curse was taking hold of her at the first jerk of her shoulder. He'd found her leaning over the railing once before, so he should have moved her away from the gallery doors immediately. He was an idiot for thinking he could talk her down. It was a fucking curse. No amount of medication, talk, or therapy could save her. He'd never felt more helpless in his life.

He fisted his hands in his lap and tapped his foot. Goosebumps pricked at his skin, so he crossed his arms to chase away the chill. Hospitals were always so damn cold.

"Eric Landry?" A man's voice pulled him from his thoughts, and he looked up to find a police officer addressing him.

"That's me." He uncrossed his arms and straightened his spine, his pulse taking off like a racehorse. *Oh, god, Trish.* No, Trish was fine. If she wasn't, they'd have sent a doctor to break the news.

"I'm Officer Theriot. I need to ask you a few questions about your wife's fall." He sat in the chair across from him. Officer Theriot had broad shoulders, a barrel of a chest, and dirty blond hair styled into a crew cut.

Eric's hands returned to their fisted position. Surely they didn't think he...

"Where were you when she went over the railing?"

Holy shit. They did. "I was in the bedroom. By the time I made it onto the gallery, she had already fallen."

"Did you and your wife have an altercation? An argument of some kind?"

This was unreal. "We were having a discussion," he said through clenched teeth. "If you're trying to insinuate that I pushed her over, I didn't. I love her. I would *never* hurt her."

"Eric! How's Trish?" His grandma rushed to his side, sank into the chair next to him, and took his hand.

"She was coherent when they loaded her into the ambulance, but they won't let me see her." He arched a brow at the cop.

"Why not?"

"Because Officer Theriot thinks I threw my wife over the railing."

His grandma whirled to face the officer. "Marc Theriot, you know better than that. How dare you accuse my grandson of such behavior. Do I need to speak with your chief?"

Theriot's shoulders slumped, and he hung his head like a schoolboy who'd just been scolded by the headmistress. Eric fought his smile. His grandma knew just about everyone with any clout in New Orleans.

"I'm sorry, ma'am. It's standard procedure."

"Theriot." Another officer gestured for him to approach her, and she lowered her voice and said something to him when he arrived at her side.

"It wasn't the curse, was it?" his grandma asked.

"We couldn't break it. When I woke up, she was panicked. She kept talking about whispers, and then she became frantic."

"Why did you let her onto the gallery?"

He huffed. "I didn't. I tried to stop her."

"Mr. Landry," the second officer said. "She's in room 367. You're clear to see her."

He rose. "Am I clear from the allegation?"

She nodded. "Your wife corroborated your story. She isn't pressing charges."

His brow slammed down over his eyes, but he shoved his anger at the ridiculousness down. Right now…and always…his focus needed to be on Trish. "Give me a few minutes?" he asked his grandma.

"I'll be right here."

He strode past the officers and hung a left, pacing down the hall at a fast clip. When he reached room 367, he found Trish propped up in her bed, her hands folded in her lap.

"I'm so sorry." The apology tumbled from his lips as he sat on the edge of the bed and rested his hand on hers. "I should have moved you away from the gallery. I should have recognized how bad the episode was."

What was he doing? This wasn't about him. Trish was the one lying in a hospital bed. She was the one driven to throw herself over the railing because of a stupid curse. "How are you? What did the doctor say?"

"I'll live." She offered him a small smile. "I'm scraped and bruised and sore as hell, but I'll recover. They're waiting on the radiologist to confirm I don't have any internal injuries, and then I'll get to go home."

"Thank goodness." His breath came out in a rush of relief. "What happened on the gallery?"

She stared at his hand on hers for a moment before lifting her gaze to his. "I'm not really sure. One minute, I heard whispering and saw shadows darting around me, and the next, I became panic-stricken and had to get out of the house."

He glanced at the door and lowered his voice. "Were you pushed?"

She gave her head a tiny shake. "I told the police I was leaning on it and fell over, but I…I *think* that's what happened. I don't remember." Tears gathered on her lower lids.

"Knock, knock." Natasha tapped her knuckles on the open door. "I just got back into town when I heard you took a tumble." She stepped into the room, and Trish wiped the tears from her eyes.

"I'm still cursed."

"Maybe. Maybe not." She tilted her head. "Could've been your own mind making you act that way. You've been through a helluva lot."

Trish sobbed, and a tear rolled down her cheek, breaking Eric's heart. Had the panic come from her anxiety? Was the fall truly nothing more than an accident? It pained him to think her mental health had taken a turn for the worse, but if it wasn't the curse, they could get help. She could adjust her medications, see a therapist. And he would stay by her side to help her through it all.

"Can I talk to you outside?" Natasha asked him.

"I'll be right back." He squeezed Trish's hand before following the priestess into the hall.

She gestured to the right, and they walked a few doors down, out of Trish's earshot. "I thought you said you two were married."

"We are."

She arched a brow.

"We were planning to file for an annulment as soon as the curse was lifted, but it's a legal marriage for now."

"It's a fake." She shook her head like she was disappointed. "Neither of you meant it."

Eric shrugged. "At first, I guess it was, but I mean it now. I'm in love with her."

"Mm-hmm." She crossed her arms. "Have you told her that?"

He lowered his head. "Not yet. I was planning to this morning, but…"

"You can't fool a curse, child. Your intentions weren't pure when you went into the marriage. Voodoo magic knows what's in your heart. Intention is everything."

"We thought she was getting better. Once we started acting like a couple, she seemed fine most of the time."

"That's the nature of the curse. Like I told you from the beginning, periods of relief make the manic episodes that much worse." She sighed. "I expected more from someone with your abilities."

He shoved his hands into his pockets. He expected more from himself. "Why did you just tell Trish she wasn't cursed?"

"I never said she wasn't."

"You made it sound like it all came from her mind."

She wrapped her arm around his shoulders. "Listen to me. I have your ability too, and I know you love her."

"I do. With all my heart."

"To end this curse, you have to marry her for real. Both of you have to mean it this time, and the only way to ensure that is for her to think the curse is lifted. She can't go into it thinking you're doing it because of the hex. Understand?"

"True love will break the curse." He laughed dryly. It sounded like a fairy tale.

"A *real* marriage. Based on the emotions I picked up from the both of you, I assumed that you'd mean it from the beginning. She loves you too. Has for a while now." She shook her head. "I should know better than to assume anything."

He swallowed the lump from his throat. "Got it. Thanks, Natasha."

"Good luck."

Eric paced back to Trish's room and sank onto the bed. Tears trailed down her cheeks, and he wiped them away with his thumb. "I'm sorry for all of this. I should have protected you."

"There was nothing you could have done. I'm a mess, Eric. Beyond help. I should be locked in a padded cell."

"Don't say that." He brushed a strand of hair from her forehead. "I love you."

"What?" she whispered and furrowed her brow.

The lump returned, and he swallowed it down again. "I told you I loved you last night, but you were already asleep."

More tears gathered on her lids. "I didn't hear you."

"I know, and I'm sorry I didn't say it sooner. I wanted to so many times, but I was afraid you didn't feel the same." He held her gaze, and when she didn't speak, he continued, "The truth is I'm terrified of rejection. It's the reason I don't stay in relationships long. I always leave when I can feel the women having second thoughts, so they don't have the chance to reject me. But you're different, Trish. Even if I could feel your emotions, I would never leave you. If you kicked me to the curb and told me you hated me, I still wouldn't give up. You are the only woman I want. I love you."

She laced her fingers through his. "I love you too, Eric."

His chest swelled like a can of biscuits had popped open inside it, and pressure built in the back of his eyes.

A tear rolled down her cheek. "It took me a while to realize it, but you are everything I've ever wanted. I only wish I'd seen it sooner. I'm in love with you."

"Oh, Trish." He cupped her cheek in his hand and

brushed his lips to hers. He started to pull away, but as she clutched the back of his neck and deepened the kiss, he *knew*. She put so much love into the kiss, all doubts were erased from his mind. He didn't need his ability to understand that no one in his entire life had ever felt this way about him, and he was overcome with so much emotion he could barely contain it.

As the kiss slowed, he pulled back and gazed into her eyes. "Marry me, Trish."

She smiled. "Eric…"

"Let's get married again. For real this time. I want to spend the rest of my life with you. Will you be my wife?"

"I already am." She grabbed her purse from the table and pulled out the annulment form. "How about we *stay* married. For real." She ripped the paper in half and handed one side to him. "'Til death do us part?"

"Not even then." He tore the annulment into as many pieces as he could and dropped it in the trash while Trish did the same.

"Are you saying you'll be my ghost husband?" she asked.

"If you're haunting, I'll be by your side. I love you, Trish."

"I love you too. Oh." She rubbed her chest, and her face scrunched.

"What's wrong?" He clutched her hand, his heart kicking into a sprint.

"I don't know. Something snapped, and cold spread through me. It's gone now."

Someone cleared their throat from the doorway. "Was that so hard?" Natasha asked. "*Now* the curse is broken."

Trish looked at Eric before turning to the priestess. "But you said…"

"I never said nothing. Congratulations. You two are meant to be together." She smiled. "Didn't think it'd take you this long to figure it out, but I'm glad you did. I'll see you around." She turned and left the room as Grandma Landry stepped through the door.

"I got tired of waiting," she said. "How are you, Trish?"

She squeezed Eric's hand. "Honestly, I've never been better."

CHAPTER TWENTY-TWO

*T*rish stared at her reflection in the mirror as Emily pinned a champagne-colored rose into her hair and Sydney fluffed out the train on her dress. Light brown shadow with a muted gold shimmer accented her eyes, and a soft pink gloss on her lips completed the look.

Emily stood behind her and rested her hands on her shoulders. "You look so beautiful."

"How many women get to marry the man they love twice?" Though their marriage at the courthouse was legally binding, Grandma Landry insisted they have a "proper" wedding. They all knew she wanted them to have it so she could show off to her friends, but Trish was okay with that.

She'd always dreamed of a fairytale wedding, and now that she'd figured out Prince Charming had been right in front of her for years, she was happy to go through the pomp and circumstance.

"Trish Landry does have a nice ring to it," Sydney said.

"It sure does. I already changed it on my driver's license. I get giddy every time I look at it."

"How are you feeling now?" Emily asked. "No anxiety?"

Trish focused on her body, searching for a hint of the adrenaline that could spark a panic attack. All she felt was calm. "I'm good. We knocked down the disappointments room wall and reclaimed the space. Now, I'm ready to meet the man of my dreams at the end of the aisle and tell him I'm his forever."

"Ladies," the wedding planner said from the doorway, "we're ready for you."

Trish waited outside the chapel doors as Sydney and Emily took turns walking down the aisle. Roses in shades of champagne and blush filled the sanctuary with their sweet fragrance, and two large bouquets sat on tables at the front of the room. Her friends looked gorgeous in their pale pink bridesmaids' gowns, and when the wedding march began, the planner opened both doors.

Everyone stood as Trish walked down the aisle alone. She was a grown woman, so she didn't need anyone to give her away. She was giving herself to Eric, and when her gaze locked on his hazel eyes, her chest swelled with love.

He looked handsome in his tailored black tuxedo, his hair combed perfectly into place. His smile made her pulse race, and as she reached him, she handed her bouquet of roses to Emily and placed both her hands in his.

Her gaze never strayed from his eyes as the officiant gave the "dearly beloved" speech. Her cheeks ached from smiling so big, but she couldn't have fought it if she tried.

"I believe Eric and Trish have prepared their vows," the officiant said. "Eric, you may say yours now."

Eric's smile beamed. "I love you, Trish. Honestly, I've

always loved you. I knew you were special from the moment we met, and I promise to make sure you know how much I treasure you from the time you wake up each morning, into your dreams at night, every day, for the rest of my life."

Her breath trembled as she inhaled, tears of joy gathering in her eyes. "Eric, you are the man of my dreams. You're kind, sweet, funny, and you're a helluva cook. I don't know why it took me so long to figure it out, but I promise to love you with all my heart and soul for as long as my soul exists. On this plane and the next." And she meant every word.

"Eric, do you take this woman to be your wife, to love, honor, and cherish her, in sickness and in health, as long as you both shall live?"

Eric's gaze penetrated all the way to her soul, giving her goosebumps as he said, "I do."

Then it was her turn.

"Trish, do you take this man to be your husband, to love, honor, and cherish him, in sickness and in health, as long as you both shall live?"

"Yes, I do. God, do I ever."

Their guests laughed at her response, but she didn't care. "I do" wasn't enough to describe her commitment to this man.

"By the power vested in me by the State of Louisiana, I now pronounce you husband and wife. You may kiss the bride."

"Gladly." Eric hooked one arm behind her neck, and with the other on the small of her back, he dipped her, taking her mouth in a tender kiss.

She held his face, kissing him back with everything she was worth until her friends cleared their throats, telling them enough was enough. "I love you," she said as he righted her.

"I love you too, Mrs. Landry."

God, how she loved the sound of that.

Grandma—she insisted Trish call her that now—planned an extravagant reception in a hotel ballroom, complete with an open bar, a band, and a dancefloor, where she and Eric spent most of their time.

They stood cheek to cheek, swaying to the music, and she lost herself in his embrace. Emily had to drag her away to toss the bouquet, which one of Eric's cousins caught after nearly knocking down the other women to get to it.

The limo arrived to whisk them away to their honeymoon, and as they prepared to leave, Grandma pulled them aside. "I want you to open my gift now." She handed Eric an envelope.

"You didn't have to get us anything." Eric winked as he opened it. "Trish is all the gift I need." His eyes widened as he stared at the document inside.

"Thank you." He hugged Grandma before handing the paper to Trish. "I told you I'd make all your dreams come true."

Her hands trembled as she stared at the page. "This is the deed to the house."

"In both your names. A wedding gift, as it was always intended to be."

"Thank you." Trish tried to shake her hand, but she pulled her into an embrace.

"In this family, we hug." She squeezed her tightly before patting her back. "Y'all better scoot. You don't want to miss your plane."

Their friends and guests blew bubbles as they walked between them to the car, and Eric opened the door for her before climbing in beside her and lacing his fingers through hers.

"We're homeowners now." He kissed her cheek.

"My dream home. My dream man. It wasn't easy to get here, but I'd do it all over again if it meant I'd end up with you."

ALSO BY CARRIE PULKINEN

Crescent City Wolf Pack Series

Werewolves Only

Beneath a Blue Moon

Bound by Blood

A Deal with Death

A Song to Remember

Shifting Fate

Crescent City Ghost Tours Series

Love & Ghosts

Love & Omens

Love & Curses

New Orleans Nocturnes Series

License to Bite

Shift Happens

Life's a Witch

Santa Got Run Over by a Vampire

Finders Reapers

Swipe Right to Bite

ALSO BY CARRIE PULKINEN

Haunted Ever After Series

Love at First Haunt

Second Chance Spirit

Third Time's a Ghost

Stand Alone Books

Sign Steal Deliver

Flipping the Bird

Azrael

The Rest of Forever

Bewitching the Vampire

Soul Catchers

ABOUT THE AUTHOR

Carrie Pulkinen is a paranormal romance author who has always been fascinated with things that go bump in the night. Of course, when you grow up next door to a cemetery, the dead (and the undead) are hard to ignore. Pair that with her passion for writing and her love of a good happily-ever-after, and becoming a paranormal romance author seems like the only logical career choice.

Before she decided to turn her love of the written word into a career, Carrie spent the first part of her professional life as a high school journalism and yearbook teacher. She loves good chocolate and bad puns, and in her free time, she likes to read, drink wine, and travel with her family.

Connect with Carrie online:
www.CarriePulkinen.com

Made in the USA
Las Vegas, NV
09 April 2022

47123527R00152